OTHER BOOKS

Two Nights of Courage
Jeep
Cast you Nets
What If
Grunt, Brute and The Lady
Family Ghosts
Cameo
Mary, Mary

FATHER JON SERIES

Wipe My Tears
Not My Legs
The Lady of Perpetual Peace
The Shepherd's Heart
To the Ends of The Earth

Constance

GROWING UP

PENELOPE S. HESSION

THE HOLY BIBLE, NEW INTERNATIONAL VERSION®, NIV® Copyright © 1973, 1978, 1984, 2011 by Biblica, Inc.® Used by permission. All rights reserved worldwide.

ISBN: 978-1-6847-0725-6 (sc)
ISBN: 978-1-6847-0724-9 (e)

Lulu Publishing Services rev. date: 07/02/2019

This book is dedicated to
Jesus Christ, my healer, who miraculously restored
my eyesight when I was going blind.

Jesus said:
This is why I speak to them in parables:
"Though seeing, they do not see;
though hearing, they do not
hear or understand.
In them is fulfilled the prophecy
of Isaiah:
"You will be ever hearing but
never understanding;
you will be ever seeing but
never perceiving.
For this people's heart has
become calloused;
they hardly hear with their ears,
and they have closed their eyes.
Otherwise they might see with
their eyes,
hear with their ears,
understand with their hearts
and turn, and I would heal them."

Matthew 6:13-15, NIV

And personal thanks to the following:
Patrick, Chet, and James
Friends and encouragers extraordinary

Constance

The rough hand covered her mouth before she was able to scream. Constance was at her favorite game, hiding from those who were hunting her from the castle. She played it whenever she was bored which was often. Rain or snow sometimes cut the game short but the caloused hand surprised her in roughness and strength. She reasoned, to herself, I am the Princess!" She twisted and wrestled. He held her closer as the briars thorns also latched on to her skin and clothing. She wrinkled up her nose as her captor pulled her closer.

She almost missed the sounds of horses of the search party as they came around the bend in the road ahead, she tumbled into the mass of bushes in the in her hurry to disappear. "Psssh", a voice quietly spoke close to her ear. "You really don't want them wat them to find you."

A brief gasp for air was followed by the large hand again covering her mouth. She was faint and fearful. She had no strength left

Usually, Constance enjoyed the prestige of never being corrected even when she played hard to find for the couriers of the court. When they brought her back and presented her, often with torn clothing and dirty, her father just dismissed her as being a nuisance and returned to whatever pleasure he was pursuing at the time.

Quietly, she awaited their passing as they had not seen her quick movement and the restraining hand. After they passed, she tried to untangle herself from the prickly bush. "Ouch," she said aloud. A large hand again covered her mouth.

"Ssssh," a man's menacing voice came close to her ear. "You don't want them to hear you and turn back, and neither do I."

She struggled against the strong hands that held her tightly. "You are a devil of a person to hold on to," he said after a while in a low voice.

She looked at him. "You are nothing but a highwayman!" She attempted to pull herself away only to find herself more entangled.

"Hold still," he said as he covered her mouth with one hand and used the other one to remove the prison of briars that held her.

"I have a notion to just leave you here stuck tight in the briars," the man grunted when he had mostly freed her. She had tried to break away from his grasp and entangled them both more of the prickly thorns.

"You wouldn't dare," the young girl had managed to twist from under the restraining hand covering her mouth.

"Don't tempt me," he reapplying his hand over her mouth.

Every so often one pointed thorn would stick into her skin. She would have screamed but for the restraining hand covering her mouth.

"I am the King's daughter," she got the words out after biting the hand covering her mouth.

"You do that again, and you will be a very sorry King's daughter," he said as at last her pulled her from the briars. "Now get one thing straight, you are in my possession and you will do what I say."

For all of her pretended fierceness, Constance felt afraid. The man was strong. "You will get death," she bragged "when they find me with you."

He nodded.

Death was something he was living with anyway. "Not if I return you to the King in the throne room."

"A highwayman getting into the throne room!" She would have laughed a shrill laugh had he not clamped his hand over her mouth again.

"The undisciplined King's daughter," he said as he tucked her under his cloak and made his ways through the rapidly darkening forest.

When she tried to cry, his grip intensified and she found pinned tightly to his side. He was wearing some sort of armor! There was nowhere to sink her teeth into flesh.

"Who are you?" she managed that she could scarcely breath.

"You are determined to learn discipline," he said to her roughly.

Feeling faint from the suffocating grip under his cloak, Constance said nothing.

His footsteps stomped through water. He set her down so suddenly that she nearly fell on the slippery rocks. It was dark.

"Where are we?" she asked as she teetered before his strong arm caught her.

"Stand still," he said. His voice had an echo to it. Minutes later he had a lit candle. The eerie shadows frightened. her.

"We are in a cave," she gasped.

"Cold?" he asked as her shivered.

She nodded.

He threw his cloak over her shoulders. The armor he was wearing glittered in the candlelight.

"Who are you?"

"Do you recognize the crest?"

Constance squinted her eyes in the dimly lit cave.

"Well," he said, keeping his voice gruff. "Surely you are not that ignorant."

"What are you doing in the crest of my father!" The laugh that met her challenge scared her. "Who are you?"

"You will make a regal queen if you are disciplined," he said under his breath. "So much like your mother, God rest her soul."

"How dare you talk about my mother!"

"Little, spoiled princess, playing your games, running away and hiding. The days are growing short, it is time you grow up."

"You haven't answered me," she said and stomped her foot forgetting the slipping rocks under her feet.

He quickly moved keep her from falling into the stream of the cave.

"What are you doing? Let go of me," she demanded.

As tempted as he was, he didn't. She would have been soaked to the skin and he didn't have anything to put on her if she got wet. Instead, he pinched her on her backside.

"Ow!" she responded. "Why did you do that?"

"Merely a warning, my dear, a warning of discipline. "Much to the surprise of both of them, she had no response.

He wrapped her in his cloak before he picked her up and carry her deeper into the cave. She clung to his neck hoping he would he did not drop her and leave her there. It seemed that he had walked for miles before he sat her down on some animal skins and reclined beside her. "We will sleep now."

"I am hungry."

"When we get up," and he snuffed the candle.

He felt her trying to get up. He placed a hand firmly on her.

Fear gripped Constance. She had never encountered anything like this before. She whimpered.

"Shush," he said and she felt the sting of a pinch. She lay very still hoping he would go to sleep.

When Constance woke, the candle was lit. "Come, we have a long way to go," he said to her. When he touched her shoulder, she screamed. "None of that," and he made a move to pinch her. She tried to scramble away. "First lesson, don't run from me." He pulled her back and gave her a sharp pinch. When she struggled, he repeated it. Her eyes grew big as the second one was sharper than the first.

"I see you understand."

"Let me introduce myself to you. I am your uncle, Daniel."

"The murderer!" she gasped.

"It all depends on who is telling the story," he said.

"There is a bounty on your head. You will never get away with keeping me." Her defiance of him was almost laughable.

"What are you going to do, run away, play your childish game?" He reached over and she scooted back. "You have forgotten already, haven't you? He pulled her to him and pinched her not once but twice. The second one much more painful than the first.

Constance sat very still for a moment before launching herself straight at him. He did not let her get far before she was subdued. He repeated the pinches with a third one sustained. She cried in anguish.

"Enough?" She nodded as tears ran down her face.

They left the cave through a narrow gap the opened into a field. Across the meadow sat a stone barn and a small cottage. Daniel, as her uncle finally instructed her to call him, whistled. A short time later, a horse was released from the barn. When the animal came nearer, she wondered at its splendor and built. From a small hut, Daniel retrieved a saddle and bridle.

"The horse is beautiful." she said in awe as Daniel prepared the horse for riding.

"I understand that the princess is a daring rider."

Constance stared at him. "Who told you?"

He nodded toward the barn and house across the meadow. "He has heard of your daring even on the stallions that are used in the games. You ride like a lad, not a lass."

"It is dumb to ride like a lass. One misstep and you are on the ground."

"Not very lady-like though," he said as he prepared to mount the now fully ready horse. "So, you will not find it difficult to ride in front on me like a lad then, at least until we get near the castle."

"You are taking me there?" He lifted her up onto the saddle and mounted the horse behind her.

"Weren't you afraid that I would take off on this horse by putting me up here first?"

Daniel's voice came from behind her. "Remember, you are in a might poor place to attempt to antagonize me." He rested his hand lightly on her before urging the horse into a fast walk toward the far end of the meadow.

Constance felt a shiver of dread from his nearness behind her.

For a long time, they traveled across many fields and on lesser-used roads as Daniel urged the horse to keep a steady pace toward the castle. Stopping at a small farmhouse, Daniel asked for some food. Soon they were sitting in the shelter of the woods, eating. Constance was glad to be down on the ground, away from Daniel's restraint. She was tired of the constant steady pace.

"Why don't we gallop?" she asked. "I am sure your horse would like the change of pace."

"And so, would you little Miss dare devil."

"I am not!" she retorted.

Her uncle looked at her long and hard. "We will be there soon. They know we are coming now. We should be meeting them soon. Come on, up you go," and without ceremony, Daniel lifted her into the saddle. He was up in a flash behind her.

True to his words, other riders wearing the same crest as Daniel met them at the next crossroad. Several nodded and swung in behind them and beside them.

"Are they guarding us or protecting us?" Constance said over her should to Daniel.

"A little of both," he answered. "As a wanted man with a bounty on my head, I need protection and then again, you need protection because I have you in my custody. Call it insurance for a safe passage to the throne." Daniel chuckled.

Constance was thinking about what she had heard about her uncle. He was wanted for murder but she couldn't remember who had been murdered. She knew that her father hated him. "Aren't you the oldest?" she asked.

Daniel tightened his grip with his legs on the horse. Sensing the tension, the horse's ears were alert. "Yes," he said at last and relaxed his body as they were now within sight of the castle. He reined in the horse. "It is always a beautiful sight in the late afternoon light."

The others stopped close around Daniel and Constance. "Why did you stop?" she asked.

"I am waiting for the right moment," Daniel said. "Swing your leg over and ride like a lady."

"Why?"

"Because I told you," was followed by a hard pinch. Constance thought of making a scene but elected to obey. "Good girl," Daniel said in a low voice.

"Now!" one of the other horsemen said. As one unit, the group moved at a trot towards the open gate of the castle. Constance was hanging on to Daniel as they entered the gate. The first horseman, rode straight into the building followed by all the rest. They stopped at the back of the throne room, eight abreast

"What is the meaning of this," a voice was shouting from somewhere near the throne.

Daniel moved his horse one step forward. "I have brought back your missing daughter, Constance, as ransom for my life," he shouted toward the throne.

Constance saw her father, the King. He looked frightened.

"You kidnapped her?"

"No, she literally fell into my hands in a briar bush."

Constance struggled to free herself from Daniel's grip on her to no avail. "You didn't have to tell him that," she hissed.

"Is that true?" her father asked as a crowd of spectators milled about the open doors of the throne room.

"Answer him," Daniel said to her. His grip had tightened on her.

"Yes, Father."

"Put her down."

"Not until I am given your pledge of acceptance of her in return for my life."

Constance tried to squirm out of his grip again. Her effort was met by a sharp pinch on her backside.

Various factions of the court now organized themselves at the ready for what would happen next. Many were torn with the desire for the banished Daniel to be returned to the court. Others were afraid of the bloodshed that might erupt at any moment.

In the middle of the tension was the heir-apparent, the princess Constance who was being held by Daniel. It was obvious to many that he was physically holding her in front of him as a ransom for his life. In fact, they had rarely seen the young girl in the royal court or as silent as she was at present.

"I accept your offer," the King said, "although I wonder why," he said aside to those closest to him. "She is nothing more than a nuisance."

Daniel did not move. Constance thought he would let go of her. Her first movement by was met with another pinch. She sat quietly.

"Swear it," Daniel spoke out.

There was an audible gasp in those watching. The two brothers glared at each other.

"I swear it." The King tried the easy way out.

"Say the words that will release me from the death bounty." Daniel waited.

After a moment's hesitation, and following the prompting of someone standing near him, the King said, "I swear that you, Daniel, are no longer under the death bounty and are a free man subject to all the privileges of a free man, so help me god." Those who were often in the throne room with him on business noted the fact that he faltered several times and had to be prompted.

One of the other men on horseback moved to the middle of the room. "You have heard the decree. Go and spread the word. Prince Daniel is no longer a wanted man."

During the ensuing applause and sounds of exclamation, the King and his consorts departed the room.

Daniel released his hold on Constance. "Go to your private chambers and stay there."

As she was assisted in her dismount, she looked at her uncle. "Will I see you again?"

Daniel laughed. "Yes, my princess." The crowd clamored in around him.

Someone took her hand to safely get through the crowds. She retired to her rooms where her attendants tended to her briar cuts and scratches.

At Home Again

The noises outside her chamber filtered into her dreams. She often fought the efforts of her ladies to get her up and properly dressed.

Each time an attendant approached the bed, Constance pulled the covers over her head. Although she could very well hear their pleas, she chose to ignore them. She was dreaming or was it imagining her next game of playing 'hide and seek' with them. She The cave where she had spent the night with her capturer, her uncle Daniel, was a perfect place to stay if the weather got nasty. She imagined entering it from the meadow where they had come out, fooling those hunting for her. In her mind, she did not consider that her uncle would know where she was when they reported that she had disappeared without a trace.

A disturbance brought her wider-awake. It sounded like a man in her outer chamber. No man was allowed in the room so her ears must be playing tricks on her. She rolled over taking her covers with her in readiness to hide from her attendants.

Suddenly a male voice spoke in her bedchamber. "What do you mean she is not up?" She puzzled over the familiarity of the sound, she scooted down deeper in the bed. "Get her up!"

"Daniel?" Another attendant attempted to get her to open her eyes. Constance pulled her covers over her head.

"Does she have any clothing on?" the male voice asked.

"Oh, yes, sire," the frightened attendant replied. That was the only warning she had before the bed covers were torn from her hands and she lay exposed. Constance was so surprised that she opened her eyes.

Her uncle dropped the covers on the floor. His next move was to lift her from the bed and stand her on her feet in front of him. The attendants expected a scream, for they had tried that tactic themselves once or twice with no results. "Get her suitable clothes for the throne room," her uncle ordered.

"You will be dressed and ready when I return," he said. It was like no one else was in the room as his eyes bored into hers. "And you will not make a sound or resist their attention to you." He lifted his hand slightly and moved with his fingers together as though he was going to pinch her.

"No," she yelled both in rebellion to the order and the anticipated pinch.

With his other hand he dismissed her attendants before he calmly pinched her. "You will learn discipline," he said and turned to walk out.

Constance stood in amazement at the boldness of her uncle to enter her private chambers and then to treat her so harshly. The sting from the pinch remained as a reminder. She could not ignore as her attendants helped her dress.

She had barely completed her personal tasks as well as submitting to the elaborate dress that was being put on her when she heard her uncle's voice in the anteroom and several other male voices. Neither her attendants nor she could not make out what they were saying.

The two women helping looked with approval when their task seemed finished. The door opened.

Constance hated the garment she had on. It always meant hours of sitting in the throne room while some stuffy visitor spent all his time talking with her father.

"Why are her arms bare?" Constance whirled around to stare at her uncle. "Get the seamstress to make sleeves for her immediately. She is no longer a little girl!"

"What are you doing in my private chamber?" If she had to wear this despicable dress, she was going to act like a princess. She ordered the offending male out.

Daniel's hand signal was clear to the two waiting ladies and they exited. "Sit down my princess and listen."

Dumbfounded, she sat in the chair he indicated.

"During the night, your father, the King, died."

For a twelve-year old who had very little reference and contact with her father, the King, the words went in and stopped. The depth of the meaning of her father's death was not something she could understand. "You are lying," she replied.

Daniel was looking down at the floor. "You are now the potential ruler of the Kingdom. And," he said after a pause, "you have no discipline or training."

Outside the room the ladies in waiting strained their ears to hear what Daniel was saying. They knew of the events of the night. It had not come as a surprise. The stories that circulated before dawn were that the two men had talked late into the night, and sometime after Daniel had left his brother's private chambers, one of the King's consorts had reported the King was dead.

Constance looked up her uncle, the man who had pulled her out of the briars, the man who pinched her every time she acted up.

She scoffed at the thought of being the queen!

"If I am the potential queen, then who are you to treat me with so much distain."

Constance never connected that she would be the Queen.

"I am your guardian, and you will surely need one for there are many who would tell you lies and fondle you to get power."

Constance pondered her uncle's words. She had heard the rumors when others thought she was just playing nearby or planning her next runaway games. She had known that no one paid much attention to her or her father even though he was the King. It didn't mean anything.

"You will refer to me as Sire in the throne room and Uncle Daniel in private."

After he had heard of his brother's death, he had thought of the need to establish a ritual with the young princess, one in public, and the other one when they were in private.

"My father," Constance had been silent for a few minutes, "Did you kill him?"

"No," Daniel paused as he thought of what to say next. "There were others who were waiting to do that."

"Did you tell them to kill him?" She suddenly felt frightened of her uncle as he studied her face carefully.

"No." And he thought of how many times he had argued with the others not to do anything rash. "It was." He stopped. "I don't know that he was killed, maybe he just died."

"His court hated him," Constance said quietly. "I have heard talk when they not did think I was listening."

"Princess," Daniel was looking straight at her. "Let us let someone else bring up that idea."

She looked down at her hands that she had folded in her lap. "I shall say that I am sad he is dead."

There was the glimmer of the future queen in the young girl.

Daniel whispered, "Long live the princes and queen!"

There were only three days of mourning for the deceased king. Of course, the people came by the bier, as was their obligation. They barely glanced at the dead man. Some discretely made negative hand signals as the passed by. Others coughed or said things under their breath.

It was obvious that the only ones who really cared that he was dead were his consorts who sat quietly a few feet away with handkerchiefs to their eyes while they pondered their fate. It was something none of them had considered when he courted their flattery. That he would have died so soon had not crossed their minds as he showered them with fine garments, jewels, and perfumes in return for their service. The Royal Legion had placed them under guard at the instant it was confirmed that the King was dead. Daniel was now openly leader of the Legion that had long been secretly supportive of him even   during his banishment. The women pondered the justice that he might give to them for unlike his brother, they knew he was a moral and just man.

The church was filled with dignitaries from a few of the surrounding kingdoms. Few were of any merit and no direct royal families. Constance sat with her uncle behind an ornately carved screen where they could see but those in the church proper could not get a good view of them. She did not cry. Daniel mostly studied the rich symbolic furnishings of the church. The consorts were not present.

When her father was lowered into the crypt next to her mother, Constance turned her head away. Inside, she felt lost and scared. She pretended that it was just the King being buried, not her father. Daniel caught the hard look on her face. He wondered what she was thinking.

The throne room had been buzzing quietly as those there discussed the now deceased King and if his so recently restored brother would demand the throne. "Don't forget Princess Constance," someone said. There was a twitter of laughter.

"Sssh, Daniel is coming."

"Who is that he has with him?"

"The child," someone said in distain.

The room was silent when Daniel and Constance entered. Daniel escorted her to the place of honor as the heir of her father. There were sounds of feet quietly shuffling as everyone tried to get a look at the princess.

"Look at how she is dressed."

Daniel waited until Constance was settled in the oversized chair that her father had sat in before he turned to those assembled. He was wearing the family crest and slowly those in the room were aware of how many others in the room were also declaring their loyalty by the crest. The cape that the seamstress had fashioned for Constance also had the crest.

"Long live Princess Constance!" Daniel's voice echoed off the vaulted walls. The response was immediate as those in the throne room began to repeat those words over and over. Those who had been loyal to Daniel during his banishment surged forward to form a wall of protection around Constance and him.

Constance felt fear and then pride as the cheering went on. Daniel had told her this would happen. She had practiced the words she would say when they quieted down. She looked at her uncle and for a brief moment felt sadness for him. He had told her that he would not take the throne that rightfully belonged to her but would assist her in learning how to become Queen. It really didn't make much sense to her, but secretly, she was glad.

"Princess," she heard him say to her. Constance realized the people were waiting for her to say something. For a moment, she panicked. Daniel offered her his hand as he knelt in submission to the throne. She took it and stood, just a mere child.

"I am sad that the King is dead." She felt the squeeze Daniel gave her hand telling her to pause. There were those in the room who wondered if

Daniel had given her those words, and others amazed at her poise. "I am but a child, so my Uncle Daniel will reign in my place until I am of age." She sat back down.

A ground swell of noise came forth from those in the room. When it sorted itself out, most were cheering and smiling at their good fortune that Daniel had returned just in time.

"Long live Daniel," the chant began. Soon the news would be all over the Kingdom.

A phalanx of loyal men formed around Daniel and Constance kept them separated from the crowd. Constance stood and allowed Daniel to take the royal seat. The cheers echoed through the countryside as the people voiced their approval.

The first thing the new reigning King did was to give to himself a distinctive title. "I will be called The Royal Queen's Chancellor as I represent the future Queen until she is of age. He was thinking of days in the future when Constance was of age. If she wanted him to help her, a ready-made title would be useful. The people would be accustomed to the name of Chancellor by then.

In the weeks that followed, he busied himself with the necessary changes and preparations for his coronation. He decreed that the time of preparation for his coronation would be followed by three days of celebration.

As for his brother's consorts, he called them before him and gave the women two options, or rather three. They could repent and seek sanctuary in the church, leave the kingdom to live in exile or ... It was quite clear that the third option was what normally would have happened to them when they no longer had the protection of their lover. It was a quiet and somber meeting. Two sought the church sanctuary while five accept the escort to the border of the kingdom.

Privately, Daniel ordered a massive renovation of the palace to enlarge Constance's chambers, and provide for extra rooms to be added to his living areas for private meetings with certain members of the court. Even before his banishment, he had never thought it was proper for all business to take place in the throne room. It was too open and more suitable for special events.

During this time, Constance spent hours being fitted into new dresses with sleeves. A tall thin matron came daily to teach her the rudiments of basic etiquette. She knew them already but preferred her way for most things. Occasionally Daniel would send for her and drill her. Those sessions were always dramatic as she deliberately did things wrong or just made a scene to get the session over with. Daniel showed remarkable patience whereas that the matron who gave her scathing lectures about her behavior did not. Constance hid when the matron came. It worked once, and then Daniel gave her a lesson in discipline and pain just before the matron was due. The woman was amazed at Constance's demur that day.

Constance learned that Daniel's horse was now permanently housed in the royal stables. She went often to admire the horse and dreamed of riding him. Daniel had been busy nearly daily. Constance sometimes sat in the throne room when there was someone of interest but the activity didn't impression her or satisfy her sense of adventure.

It had been an exhausting day. When Daniel sent for Constance to make an appearance. She failed to appear. He should have suspected that she was plotting some adventure of her own.

She slipped away from her ladies and found the horse she had ridden with Daniel when he had returned to the palace. No one stopped her when she fed it some extra feed. Then, she quietly led it out to the paddock attached to the royal stable.

The horse seemed to sense the desire of the girl and stood very still when she stopped it by the mounting rock. Pulling herself up on the bareback of the horse, she leaned down on the arched neck of the splendid animal and whispered in his ears. With a laugh and a quick kick of her heels in his side, she urged the horse into a gallop. Clutching the mane with one hand and the halter rope with the other, she held to the horse's neck. The stable hands, aware of the horse traveling at top speed within the paddock, opened the gate before the horse swerved at the restriction. At a full gallop the horse managed to safely leave the paddock and crossed over the bridge heading out into the open countryside.

Panic-stricken stable hands ran after the horse with the girl to his back. Two Royal Legion riders had just broken out of the woods high on the far side of the palace. They looked at each other and the racing horse but for an instant. "Daniel's horse!" The words got lost in the air as the spurred their steeds to intercept the running horse.

Daniel had finished what he thought was the last of the day's business when a page came. "The Princess," the page stumbled over his words, "She was in the stable with your horse!"

"Where?" Daniel shouted as he ran toward the stable area. Others were excitedly coming toward him. One jumped off the horse that he was riding, handing the reins to Daniel as he pointed to the far meadow. In the distance, Daniel could see his horse running toward the woods.

"She is on his back," someone yelled. Daniel did not have to ask who she was. He knew.

Mounted on the borrowed horse, he could see two riders crossing at an angle toward where the running horse would enter the woods. They just might get to the woods first and stop the horse from dislodging the rider with a tree trunk or branch. He urged the horse he was on to a full gallop. He saw the interception and the girl sliding off the horse to the ground. The horse was winded with its head hanging down.

Many ran on foot or on horseback toward the scene. Daniel pulled his borrowed horse up and watched. He knew the men who had stopped his horse from running into the woods. Constance appeared unhurt.

He saw the hand of one of the rescuers raise and drop quickly and heard the scream of the girl. Constance fell to the ground from the blow. Daniel closed his eyes.

"That is the Princess!" Those coming up the meadow were screaming in panic from what they had seen and heard.

It took several minutes before the crowd determined that Constance was unhurt. The horseman who struck her was wearing the crest of the kingdom. However, they dragged him from his horse with the intent to kill him.

"Daniel is coming," the cry went up and the mob effect lessened. A second rider was attempting to put his horse between the crowd and his fellow Royal Legionnaire.

Constance was on the ground crying. Several were trying to attend to her believing she was injured.

Daniel arrived. The crowd parted except for two men who were still holding the one Legionnaire to the ground. "Let him up," Daniel ordered. Looking at the battered man, he asked, "Are you hurt?"

The blood running from his nose and cuts on his face were evident. "No, Sire."

The crowd stood there amazed. Daniel then turned to where Constance was weeping. "Get up."

"It doesn't make sense. He didn't go to her first!" the murmuring started.

Constance had not moved from the ground although she had stopped crying.

"Go back," he said to the crowd, "and say nothing about what you have seen. She fell from my horse."

The crowd turned to walk back toward the palace. "What is this?" they questioned among themselves. But they grew strangely silent as the got closer to the royal palace. Several had looked back and saw Constance on her feet. Daniel was at her side.

"Look at him," Daniel ordered. "He came to your rescue, and that was his reward."

"He hit me," she said in a faint voice.

Daniel nodded. "Discipline and pain."

The princess was hurting from the blow she had received. It didn't seem fair. "Why?" she asked.

"Go back to your quarters," Daniel said to the two men. "Take the extra horses with you." The men, so dismissed, left leading the borrowed horse and the winded horse slowly behind them.

It was growing dark. Suddenly Constance felt frightened standing at the far edge of the royal meadow so near the woods with only Daniel. He started walking toward the woods. "Where are you going?" she asked in near panic.

"We are going into the woods." He realized that she had not moved. "I don't think the future queen is going to want her kingdom to see what happens when a little girl steals a horse and nearly runs it into the ground."

"No," she wailed as he took her by the wrist.

Later, he carried her back to the palace in his arms, his heart hurting nearly as badly as she was hurting.

Discipline

Several Royal Legionnaires fell in step along their leader as he neared the Castle. One question loomed in their minds. Constance moaned as her uncle shifted her weight to climb the few steps to the entrance. Almost collectively, they let out with a sigh of relief. Those who had returned from the far meadow had said nothing but were obviously very frightened.

Nodding to two of the men, Daniel said, "Come with me," as he entered the portal. He made straight for his chambers still carrying his niece in his arms. "No one enters without my permission," he said at the door of the chambers. The two men took their positions on either side of the doorway. The silence in the castle was heavy and solemn. All were waiting on word about the Princess.

After placing Constance on a bed in a room adjoining his private ones, he summoned one of the men. "Watch over her."

The Legionnaire wondered if that meant guard her or take care of her. The one he could do well, but caring for the spoiled Princess was another thing.

Daniel pounded on the doors to Constance's rooms. The sound sent the women inside scurrying to various parts of the apartment. The doorkeeper with fear and hesitancy opened the doors. Daniel had always walked in, mostly unannounced. "Everyone who is in here, come!" His voice seemed menacing to most of them. From various parts of the Princess' private chamber, the women came to the room where Daniel stood looking like he could kill them all.

When the women were assembled, Daniel maintained his silence for several minutes. The youngest of the ladies fainted from fear.

"Leave her there," he said when one moved to help her.

"Who has known the princess the longest?" Without turning their heads or bodies, they seemed to isolate the oldest lady from the rest of them. Daniel faintly remembered the woman from when he was young.

"Your name?"

"Giselle, Sire"

"You will do," he said. "Come with me." She bowed in readiness to obey. "The rest of you," his hard eyes seemed to look into the soul of each one, "I will deal with you later."

"Come, Giselle," Daniel stepped through the door and the older woman followed him obedience. He hurried through the corridors to his own chambers. He nodded at the Legionnaire standing alert at the door before he took the older woman inside and closed the door behind them.

In Constance's quarters, the women were quietly talking about the strange visit. "And not a word about the Princess." was the biggest puzzle.

"Maybe she is dead," one offered a plausible conclusion.

"Why did he take Giselle?"

Several of them were seated and cried softly.

Once inside the private chambers, Giselle was wondering the same things. Or maybe he was going to make an example of her before disciplining the others for letting Constance go out to the stable.

"In here," Daniel opened the door. The Legionnaire felt relief that the girl had not awakened while he was on watch with her. She had moaned a couple of times but was mostly silent. Giselle looked at the silent Princess and detected several wounds even in the dim light of the room.

"No one but myself, and you, Giselle, and the Legionnaire are to come into this room for any reason. You," he turned towards the man, "will get her", he was pointing at the older woman, "what she needs and help her if she needs assistance." Daniel paused, "Take care of her, Giselle, she is going to need your care for a time." Abruptly, Daniel turned and left the room. Both adults in the room stood in silence stunned by what they saw and Daniel's words.

Giselle broke the silence. "Wait outside while I look her over."

Used to following commands, the Legionnaire left the room.

"Oh, my child, what have you come to, my little one?" Giselle gently removed the young woman's clothing piece by piece. Some parts seemed to be stuck to Constance's skin where it was wet or was it seeping from the wounds. Constance moaned but did not turn away from the gentle ministering of the woman. When she had the girl mostly undressed, she assessed what had happened to the young Princess. "You met up with someone who didn't ignore your disobedience," she whispered. She wanted to cry but there was no time now for that. She gently draped some clean sheets to cover Constance's body. Assured that wounds would not be fatal; she stepped to the door of the room and gave the Legionnaire a list of items she would need.

Constance did nothing more than occasionally moan for the next few days. She did not seem to be aware of who was caring for her. Giselle spooned soup into her and mashed cooked apples. She changed her bedding when it became soiled, and gently rubbed ointment into the worst of the wounds. Daniel came often and stood in silence, watching Giselle care for Constance.

Those of the castle were mostly silent as they worked talking only in hushed voices when they thought Daniel was not around. Two pages discussed just outside the stable door what they imagined had happened to Constance. "She was dragged by the horse into the woods, you know."

"No!" said the other. "That Legionnaire did it."

Unknown to them, Daniel overheard them. He stopped as the boys continued with their untruths. Their mouths fell open when he appeared. Members of the Royal Legion accompanying Daniel seized the boys. "Take them into the throne room. They shall be an example." Daniel pushed by them without a glance at them.

Once in the throne room, in view of members of the court, Daniel advanced in the direction of the boys. His voice thundered, "I came upon you making up stories."

"We were just talking among ourselves," one of the pages said before he was silenced by the man holding him."

"I did not give you permission to speak." Turning to the other boy and asked, "Do you wish to interrupt also?"

"No, Sire," the page whispered.

"Page Master, what do you do with insolent boys?" The master was not expecting to be asked anything and was hoping he was not going to suffer for what his charges had done. "Whip them, Sire."

"You may if you wish," Daniel said mildly. "I am a just man. Shave half of their hair off, totally. Let them continue in their positions. If that doesn't work, you may do what you wish with them."

The quieter of the two pages, bowed his head. The distinctive page haircut was evidence of the position they held. Everyone one would know they were in disgrace.

The two were dismissed from the throne room to the barber. One was still was in a strong- arm wrestling match with the man holding him.

Daniel looked at the others presence. "Princess Constance is recovering from her 'ride'. He turned and walked out.

In the Daniel's chambers, Giselle was watching the sleeping girl. "Someday, she will wake up." Daniel's voice startled her. She had not heard him enter. The woman looked at the Chancellor. *A unique name he has taken for himself,* she thought. Daniel was watching her face. "What are you thinking about? You are about as silent as the girl."

The old woman opened her mouth but said nothing.

"You are asking the question why I did it," Daniel was watching her closely.

Giselle started to shake her head.

"Don't lie," he said.

Giselle felt her face getting warm from the continual scrutinizing. "I know why," she said softly. "What I don't understand is the severity."

Daniel turned as though to leave the room.

Giselle sat down by her wounded Princess and cried. Her tears fell on the girl's face.

"You are getting her wet," Daniel said.

"Maybe my tears will help," Giselle whispered.

Daniel left,

"Did he hurt you," a small voice said from the bed.

"No, my child, I am weeping for all the pain that you have experienced. Constance! How long have you been listening?"

"When I felt something wet on my face, and then Uncle Daniel's voice."

Giselle whispered, "Thank you Lord" as she leaned down and kissed the young girl.

Constance sighed.

The old lady asked, "Did I hurt you?"

"No," she paused. "No one has ever kissed me before, like that, I mean."

After Constance had gone back to sleep, Giselle stepped out to the anteroom. She found Daniel sitting there with his head is in his hands.

"Sire?" Giselle said softly.

Daniel looked up. "I heard you talking. Is she awake?"

Giselle hesitated a moment.

"Do not be afraid to tell me," Daniel said looking intently into her face.

"We talked," Giselle said.

"Did she mention me?"

"She had heard you talking to me. She called you Uncle Daniel."

His face softened. "Thank you," he said.

New Assignment

Several days later after the Page affair that Daniel noticed only one of the boys had returned to service in the court. He called for the Page Master, who came trembling, fearful that another of the pages had stirred the Chancellor's ire.

"Where is the other boy?" He asked without any preliminaries.

"He has run away," the Page Master could barely make an answer as afraid as he was.

"Why wasn't I notified?" The irate king continued. "Did you not whip him for his misdeed?"

"Yes, Sire." The Page Master wondered what else to say. "But he broke free and ran."

"You made no effort to stop him?"

"He knocked me down, Sire."

"No one tried to stop him?" Daniel stood. The Page Master fainted at the king's movement. "Take him out," Daniel said to a couple of Legionnaires.

"Where to, Sire?"

Daniel turned his back on the man lying in a heap on the floor replied. "To his quarters."

The delirious Master was alternately wailing, weeping and mumbling in his quarters. All the pages were tiptoeing around, whispering and making up dire stories of what happened to the man in the throne room and blamed Ian and the other boy for causing the Master's collapse.

Later that day Daniel sent for Ian. When the young lad came to the private rooms of the Chancellor, he made the sign of the cross before entering the room. A lone Legionnaire led the boy to an anteroom to wait for the king.

"What is your name, boy?" The Chancellor had appeared without warning.

"Ian, Sire," the lad, answered as he made the customary bow before the king.

"Enough of that." Daniel's voice seemed menacing to Ian. "Did the Page Master take a whip to you?"

Ian's heart was racing. "No, Sire, the other boy knocked him down and ran away."

"You weren't whipped?"

Ian found the words to answer. "No, Sire."

"Then I suppose I will have to do it." Daniel answered, as he watched the lad carefully.

"Sire?" Ian had raised his eyes from the floor where he had been staring.

"Speak, Ian."

"You said you are a just man."

"I am," Daniel acknowledged.

"Your punishment was to cut my hair."

Daniel turned away to break the tension between him and the lad.

"Yes," he responded as he turned back to Ian. "Tell me about yourself."

Ian didn't know whether to be relieved or if the king was just toying with him. The former one had been notorious for saying one thing and doing the opposite.

"Well," Daniel said when the boy did not speak up quickly.

"I am from the high mountains to the north, the only son of my elderly parents. They sent me to the castle to learn something more than just tending the flocks."

"Did the Page Master pay them for you?"

Ian looked down a moment. "Yes, Sire, a small amount until I could prove myself worthy."

"Do your parents need you to help them?"

"My sisters and their families are there. They are cared for." Ian looked at the king. "Please, don't send me home, Sire." Ian involuntarily touched the stubble hair that was just beginning to grow.

Daniel sighed. The boy was obviously a sensitive young man and intelligent in speech.

"You are no longer a Page."

Ian gulped.

"You will be in service here in my quarters instead." Ian looked at the king, thinking. *What is he talking about?*

"In a few weeks, my niece, the Princess will need a companion who can protector her. If you prove you can obey and keep her from doing foolish things, which her ladies can't seem to do, your parent's will be very proud of you. She is a strong-willed young lady. Do you understand what I am saying?"

Ian nodded before he remembered to answer, "Yes, Sire." He had heard the many stories about the Princess besides her horse escapade.

"You will start your training now. When she is recovered enough, I will introduce you to her. She is living in my quarters right now. You are not to go near her room. A Legionnaire and her lady are with her always."

"And the barber will cut the rest of your hair so it all grows out evenly. I will send for your things from the Pages' Quarters." Daniel tapped on a bell and an elderly man appeared. "Show Ian his room. He can have the one in the turret."

The dismissal was obvious.

Ian bowed and left with the older man. "I am Ralle, chief of the servants in the king's quarters. I give the orders."

Ian understood the brief introduction.

He had learned not to asked questions from the Page Master. There was always a master. It was one of the most important things a person could learn to live a peaceful life, whether it was in the castle, the king's rooms, or even in the attic bedroom he had in his parents' small cottage.

The turret was small, reached by few steps off the main hallway. There were two windows in the room, one looking east and the other south. Only dust and cobwebs occupied the room. Ralle looked at the boy. "Clean the dust, I will find some things for in here."

"Yes," Ian realized he did not know how to address the man.

"Yes, master," Ralle quickly ended his doubt with a light cuff on the head. "The barber will be here shortly. No hair will be better than some hair." Ralle laughed at his joke as he left the room.

Ian went to the window that looked eastward. He could see the spires of a church. It was getting late in the day and the sunlight glistened off the polished spires. He knelt at the window and prayed. "Thank you, Lord."

A tap at the door frightened him, as he had not started to clean the dust and cobwebs. The door opened and another lad about a head taller than he entered with his few possessions from the Page's Quarters. He dropped them down on the dusty floor. The cloud of dust bellowed up sending the two young men into fits of sneezing.

"You need to clean!" Both boys laughed.

"Ralle told me to." Ian wanted to say more but another bout of sneezing stopped him.

The new boy grabbed one of Ian's page shirts and began to dust. It only made it more difficult to breath.

"What am I going to do?" The two were coughing from the dust.

"What is going on in here?" A Legionnaire was standing in the doorway.

The boys froze. "The dust, we are trying to get rid of it." The taller lad answered. Ian was holding the shirt he had been using as a dust cloth.

"Obviously not that way," the Legionnaire snapped back. "You work in the stables, don't you?"

"Yes, sire," the young man, answered.

"Do you wet down the stable dirt before you sweep it?"

"Yes, sire." The meaning was clear.

"What is your name?"

"Kait."

"And you?" the man looked at Ian.

"Ian, sire," Ian felt his heart drop as a knowing look appeared on the Legionnaire's face.

"You are the one! The barber wants you."

"And you," the Legionnaire looked at Kait, "Get the dust out of this room!"

Kait opened his mouth but shut it as quickly. He had been told to deliver Ian's belongings and then go to the stable. He was caught between two orders and either one or both were going to cause him to be disciplined. The Legionnaire led Ian to the barber. Kait shrugged his shoulders. He could already feel the discipline.

Ian was with the barber for only a few minutes before all of his head looked like it was covered with short bristly fur. He hurried back to the turret. Kait had poured water on the floor and was mopping with the soiled shirt.

"I am sorry," Ian murmured as he worked alongside his new friend.

"What for?" Kait asked.

"That you had to do this. It is my job, Ralle told me to clean it."

"It isn't your fault," Kait said as he rung out the sopping shirt that was more rag than garment now. "I was supposed to deliver your things and then go to the stable." Kait stood up from the bucket. "Can you get the rest?"

Ian nodded. "Will they?" He left the question hanging.

"Yes," Kait answered. "Pray for me."

Ian's head popped up. "You are a believer?"

"Yes, that is why I volunteered to bring your things to you. I wanted you to know. I have seen you at the Church." Kait was looking at Ian. "God be with you." He turned and left.

With a little luck, he would be in the stable when the Legionnaire returned, Ian prayed.

When Ralle reappeared with a small stool, table and candlesticks, the floor was still damp but no dust flew when he walked across it. "Put the candles on that little ledge above the windows so the rats don't get them."

"Rats," Ian murmured to himself. It cost him a sharp cuff across the side of his newly shorn head.

Late that night a slim figure crept into the room. Ian was instantly alert.

"Are you awake?"

He recognized Kait's voice.

Ian moved slightly. Kait dropped down beside him on the straw mat that served as a bed. "Here," he thrust something into Ian's hand. "Keep it safe, next to your heart." He spoke in the softest of whispers. "Someone went through my things today. They missed this, but they will be back looking for it."

"What is it?" Ian could feel its uneven edges and a cord attached.

"The priest gave it to me." Kait disappeared out of the room as softly as he had come in.

At the earliest daylight, Ian arose and took the object to the windows of the turret. It was a cross with a figure on it, a crucifix. He slipped it on over his head and hid it next to his skin. God had blessed him. He prayed for Kait. He sensed that he might never see Kait again.

Daniel sent for him early in the morning. "It is time you learn responsibility." He sent him to work beside an old man to learn to read. In the few moments when he wasn't totally immersed in learning, for the teacher was strict and allowed no laziness, he thought about his friend.

Daring Defiance

Constance was healing very well. There was barely a faint mark of bruise anywhere on her now. She was able to sit in the tiny garden on the balcony attached to her room. "When will I be able to go back to my own room?" she asked one day.

Her lady looked up from where she was doing some sewing on one of Constance's gowns. "You are growing so fast, that it is difficult to keep your garments fitting you properly.

Constance, aware that Giselle often did not answer her questions, replied. "I feel like I am being kept like a prisoner."

Giselle stared at the girl. "You are certainly on the mend. One of these days the Chancellor will notice."

Constance stood up. "Well, I am the Princess, and I think I shall go back to my own apartment." She headed back into the castle room where she had lain for weeks. "This place is getting old!"

Giselle followed her in. "You certainly have forgotten the lesson you were taught."

The girl whirled around. "Who are you to tell me that I cannot go to my own apartment?"

The older lady stopped and shrugged her shoulders. "I had prayed that you would understand why you have been in this room so long."

"Why have I?" Constance sounded like the child she had always been.

"When you walk out that door, you will know," Giselle said sadly and made no effort to stop the girl.

Constance stopped just short of the door. "Am I a prisoner?"

"Until you learn, you will always be a prisoner." The old lady sadly turned her head away. "Do you not remember the pain, the tears, and the pain?"

Constance had taken two steps back toward her caretaker. "No, I have not forgotten," she said in a meek voice. "Tell my Uncle Daniel that I want to talk with him. He hasn't been in here since I woke up."

"He is busy in the throne room this afternoon," Giselle reported after making Constance's request known to the Legionnaire who guarded the door from the outside.

"But he will come, won't he?" Constance asked.

"I pray that be so." Giselle began looking for a suitable garment for the Princess to wear when Daniel did come.

A page brought the news to Chancellor Daniel during a lull in activity in the royal court. Daniel half expected to see the daring Princess come prancing into the room in spite of the efforts of Giselle and the Legionnaire. He was pleased when the visitors retired to the guest rooms. He could take his dinner in his chambers, maybe with the Princess, he thought.

A discrete knock on the door that Giselle answered was a messenger from the Chancellor. He would have dinner with the Princess this evening.

When the message was repeated to Constance, she experienced a wave of fear. "Tonight?" she said in a squeaky voice.

Giselle was putting a dressier gown on the girl. "Stand still," she admonished.

It had never occurred to the young lady that what had happened to her had left her with a fear of her Uncle.

"What if he doesn't like my dress?" she questioned, trying to twist her head around to look in the mirror.

"He won't like it if it is torn. You have almost grown too big for this dress. I will have to consult with the dressmaker about your dresses." Giselle was amazed at the physical growth of Constance. She was beginning to fill out in places where she had been flat as a rail before.

When a servant came to the door to escort Constance to the Royal dining room in the Chancellor's chambers, she was as nervous as any young woman would be on a first meeting with the Chancellor. "What if he is still mad at me?" she asked Giselle just before the servant knocked on the door.

"If he were," Giselle said, "he wouldn't be having dinner with you." The old lady hoped that was the correct answer. "And remember how to behave properly!"

Constance giggled nervously. "I know how. It is just sometimes I don't want to!"

After she had gone, Giselle sat down and prayed for her charge. She smiled to herself thinking about Constance's words, 'just sometimes I don't want to!'

Daniel really didn't know what to expect when his niece had asked for a meeting. Having dinner alone with her would allow him to study her more closely than he ever done before. He had taken a wound in his soul when he had disciplined her two months before. It was one thing to stop errant behavior with a quick punishment correction, but to instill such a deep punishment on her had surprised him. She is nothing like I thought she would be, he mused to himself as he waited.

A small fire was burning in the fireplace closest to where the table was set. He studied the flames as they lapped around the sacrificial logs. "Sacrificial," he snorted to himself. The whole business of being a King was sacrificial! Rarely did he find time to do something that he wanted with the pressing duties of administrating the kingdom. Maybe Constance had it right, forget who you were and do what you wanted. Then he repented of that thought. He could have remained estranged to the throne and his brother, and the child but he had not chosen that. Instead, he had felt the duty to the throne and to Constance in spite of his banishment and death sentence. Daniel smiled as the log broke into two pieces when the flames consumed the middle of it. "Just like me," he whispered. "Just like me." Part of the log was still burning brightly while the other piece, well out of the reach of the flames, smoldered.

"The Princess Constance," his servant announced after escorting the girl into the room.

Daniel turned and looked at her. She definitely was still a child but her body was maturing. He hoped that her mind and will would also.

"It is good to see you, Constance," Daniel spoke. She looks almost frightened, he thought.

Constance curtsied, as she had always known how to do since a small child. "Your Lordship," she responded.

"Uncle Daniel," he replied.

A flicker of a smile darted across her face before it was lost in the fear that she had of her uncle.

He gestured toward the small table set and ready for them. "Shall we be seated?"

Constance covered the distance from where she had stood not too far inside the room. She waited as a servant pulled a chair before her to be seated. It was adjusted with delicacy so that she was now within an arm reach of her uncle.

The servants began their tasks of bring in the food and placing it within the reach of the two of them before they retired from the room.

"You look lovely," Daniel said as soon as they were alone. "Are you feeling better?" He began to serve the food as though it was the normal thing he did. "Do you want any of this?" He held the spoon poised over the bowl of mixed fruits."

Constance nodded before answering. "Yes, please. I am better," she concluded. She was not looking at him but her dish.

After he had served everything that he or she wanted of the many choices, he began to eat. Constance hesitated and surprise by the few words and his service to her.

"Eat," he commanded.

Reluctantly, she picked up her fork began pushing food around on her dish, eating small bites now and then.

"Are you not hungry?" he asked.

She hung her head with no answer.

"I spoke to you," he said quietly but with authority. "Answer my question."

"I am afraid," Constance replied.

"Of me?" Daniel laid down his fork. He was surprised at her remark. She didn't look up.

"That was a question," he prompted her.

"I will eat," she said picking up her fork and avoiding his question.

Daniel stared at her bowed head. "We will talk after we have eaten. And you will answer the question," he added as an afterthought.

After dutifully eating what was on her dish, Constance placed her fork down. Daniel had finish just moments before. He pushed his chair away from the table and more directly positioned to hers.

He saw her flinch when he moved closer. "The question," he said in a firm voice although he already knew the answer.

Constance chewed at her lips for a moment. Finally, she whispered, "Yes."

"More than before?" he parried back.

Her eyes darted to his face and away again as she nodded.

Daniel elected to accept her silent nod. "Do you know why?" He noticed the startled reaction in Constance.

"Why?" she replied.

"I am your uncle. I love you very much. And someday, you will inherit the throne."

Constance wanted to run. Daniel had his hand resting on her. Spontaneously, she tried to pull away. His hand rested even more firmly on her.

Without changing the pressure of his hand, Daniel tried to assume a more relaxed position in his chair.

"Let me tell you about what is going to happen next in your preparation for queenship. You must become a student, both by being instructed in how to behave, but also in learning all the things that a queen must know. You must know history, languages, some music and art, and in all ways the proper behavior of a queen."

"I have selected a companion for you to be with you at all times except when you are in your private chambers. He will be a student alongside you, a companion when you are in the gardens, or the stable, or anywhere else. He will see that you do not go where you are not supposed to and to protect you if you are in danger."

Constance raised her eyes to his face. "A Legionnaire?" she asked.

"No, an honest and disciplined lad just a tad older than you who is in service to me."

Again, Constance asked, "Why?"

Daniel sighed. "You are no longer a little child. Someday, you will be queen." He paused thinking of the other words that would explain why he had been so harsh with her. Really that didn't matter now. It had been done and now it was time to move on.

"Do I have your pledge to obey me?" he asked. He was staring into her eyes.

She dropped her eyes for a moment. "Are you ever going to do what you did to me again?"

"If it is necessary," Daniel almost whispered the words.

Constance looked away as fear gripped her. "Even if I pledge?"

"Even then, if you break your pledge."

She squirmed in her chair. The pain of the last two months was still very fresh in her mind.

"Do you pledge?" he asked again.

Constance knew what a pledge meant. It allowed no deviation from what she pledged under any circumstances. Pledges could lead to death. She had heard men make pledges and she knew it meant until death. She knew of a few that had been put to death because they broke their pledges. It scared her.

"I am just a child," she said softly.

Daniel turned his eyes away. "Yes, a child with a formidable future, a child who must learn how to obey under all circumstances. Unless you know that, how can you ever rule others and expect them to obey?"

Constance put her hands up to cover her face. She put her fingers in her ears so that she could close out what her uncle was saying to her.

He pulled her hands down and held them firmly. "You cannot hide."

"I am only a child," she repeated her earlier statement.

"I am your uncle and king until you come of age." Daniel responded back. "Your pledge, Constance."

In one blinding instant, Constance heard herself say 'no'. Daniel's response was not what she expected. He simply let go of her and seemed to disappear into the distance.

"Very well," she could hear his voice across the room from her. "You will remain a 'prisoner' in that room in my chambers forever, if that is how long it takes you to grow up."

Constance opened her eyes. Daniel was still seated near her. He rang the bell for his servants to come and they did. He sent her back to Giselle without looking at her again.

Giselle did not speak to Constance when she was returned as so returned

After several tries, Constance finally stopped trying to make the woman talk to her. Constance stomped around her room until she grew tired and then went to sleep.

Later in the evening, a courier came and escorted Giselle into the presence of Daniel. It was evident to Giselle that what had happened earlier weighed heavily on Daniel. She waited in silence for him to speak.

"Have you spoken to her?"

"No, my Lord."

"Has she tried to get you to speak?" He really didn't need an answer to that question; the girl would try. "Don't answer," he stopped her when she started to speak.

"May I speak?" Giselle asked.

Daniel nodded.

"Is it wise to treat her as a prisoner? What has she done to you? She is a reflection of her father may God rest his soul. She knows no better."

Daniel was listening to the words of Giselle with his eyes staring at nothing on the floor. The last statement brought his head up. "She does know what she is doing. Her 'no' to making a pledge of obedience was exact and very final."

"She is only a child, Sire." Giselle pleaded.

"With a strong will to be disobedient," Daniel completed the statement.

Giselle closed her mouth. Her shoulders sagged. "What do you want done?"

He roared. "I want her obedience!" Daniel turned away as though to close the session.

Giselle curtsied and said quietly. "My Lord, may it be as you wish."

"I did not dismiss you!"

Giselle stood trembling. "Beg your pardon, my Lord." She wondered for a moment if she was going to receive the anger Daniel had for Constance and the blows that should have fallen on the girl.

"A mere child, she is." He was pacing the floor now. "How do I get through to her?" he asked aloud.

"Not by beating her, but by loving her." Giselle stood in shock realizing she had answered his question that was not asked of her.

"How?" Daniel stopped in front of the woman.

If Giselle had not served all of her life in the castle under good and sometimes bad mistresses masters and had learned how not to show her fear when she was quaking inside, she might have dissolved into tears at that moment. "My Lord," she said in a soft voice. "Show her love and wait on her. She will give her pledge when she is sure of your love."

Daniel hesitated. "I am listening. Tell me more."

For an extended period of time, Giselle talked about ways to show love to the child. "Kiss her as you would a friend. Let her know that she is valuable to you."

Daniel thought of all the serious ways he had tried to show his love and care for her. "Sometimes, she needs to be disciplined."

"Stop her when she is wrong but don't forget to love her. Do you remember the toy bridge you built with the blocks?"

"And my brother tore it down," he responded to the almost forgotten memory.

"He was not disciplined for his behavior," Giselle continued, "but when you attacked him with the blocks, you were."

Daniel could see that afternoon clearly in his mind. He nodded. "You held me and loved me after I was disciplined."

Giselle nodded. "Your brother continued as he always did, but you learned something better from that."

Daniel sat down. "How do I love her?"

It was the middle of the night when Giselle finally returned to the rooms where she and Constance lived. The Legionnaire bid her good night and said softly, "The child is awake and afraid." Giselle nodded as she entered the room. Constance was curled in a ball, sobbing on the bed.

"Child," Giselle said softly. Constance dove into her arms.

"I thought you had abandoned me," the tearful girl got out between sobs.

"I cannot do that ever," Giselle patted her.

"Uncle Daniel hates me!" Constance spewed out. "He said he was going to keep me as a prisoner in this room for life!"

The older woman noted two things in what the girl was saying. She was calling the King by the name he had instructed her to call him in private and she had quoted him probably accurately. "He does not hate you, Constance. He loves you very much."

The girl was shaking her head no. "I cannot give him a pledge of obedience if he hates me."

"A pledge to the ruler has nothing to do with whether he likes you or not, my child. And your Uncle Daniel does not hate you."

As if stuck on the idea, Constance repeated herself again. "I cannot give him a pledge of obedience if he hates me."

"You did not listen to what I said." Giselle felt the girl trying to pull away. "No, you don't," and the woman held her closer. "Why can you not accept his love?"

There was no answer from the mute girl.

"Go to bed, we will talk in the morning."

Tentatively, Constance asked. "Promise?"

"Yes," Giselle whispered in the girl's ear and kissed her gently as the girl lay down on her bed. Pulling the covers up snug to the girl, Giselle paused and brushed another kiss over the hair of the girl. "Sleep well, my child."

Giselle lay down on her own bed, exhausted but unable to sleep. She prayed until somewhere between the words that ran through her mind, she also fell asleep.

Education of A Child

C onstance's life became very busy. Daniel was not in a hurry to let her go back to her own private chambers. In the mornings, Monsieur came to teacher her French, the language of diplomacy at the time. He went away daily muttering about L'enfant who could not seem to master the accent.

Mademoiselle came next. She was tall, slender with a hooked nose. Constance found her drills on the French words boring and deliberately butchered them. Mademoiselle had a short pointer that she used alternately to point at the object she wanted Constance to name in French, and to whack it across Constance's knuckles when she failed. Her parting remark daily was always, "O Mon Dieu!" with her hand over her heart. Giselle watched her charge and knew that eventually things would come to breaking point.

Afternoons were spent with the seamstress who was making a new and variety of gowns for the young girl. "Keep in mind," Giselle offered one afternoon, "that the princess is growing up and her body is changing shape."

The seamstress grunted a reply and loosened a seam that wasn't right.

"Why do I have to stand here every day?" Constance was exceptionally fidgety today. The seamstress wasn't above giving Constance a pinch whenever the girl was too restless. "Oh!" she cried out when the woman pinched her side to get her to stand still.

"Princess, stand still until she is done." Giselle admonished.

Daniel came into the chamber. "That looks lovely on you," he said with enthusiasm.

"You don't have to stand here every afternoon being push, prodded and pinched." Constance started to pull away from the seamstress. Another pinch by the woman made Constance angry. "Tell her to stop pinching me!"

"Maybe you would prefer that I pinched you instead,"

Daniel's voice was low and menacing.

Constance glanced at him with fear. "No."

The seamstress stood very still. She had forgotten herself when she pinched the princess in the Chancellor's presence. "My Lord," she said with a bow, "it is difficult to sew when she moves all the time."

"I will leave," he replied acknowledging the woman's need for singular cooperation with the child. He remembered sessions with the seamstress when he was a child and he had not been easy to work with either.

Giselle should have recognized the symptoms in the young girl. Constance became very quiet almost to the point that one could have wondered what she was planning. When Mademoiselle arrived the next morning, Constance was waiting.

"Bon jour, Constance," the haughty lady intoned. Constance hesitated just for a brief moment before she said with her hand over her heart, "O Mon Dieu!" with all the sarcasm she could muster.

Mademoiselle's reaction to the mockery was a slap across Constance's face. The scream from the girl brought Giselle running from the other room. It was obvious that she had been slapped from the red handprint on her face.

"Madam, what have you done?"

The French woman stood shaking with anger and a growing awareness of what she had done. The girl was a princess! Snatching her small bag that contained the hated pointer stick and the book from which she was teaching Constance, she bolted for the door.

It was opened by the Legionnaire who blocked her quick escape. He looked first at the sobbing princess and then Giselle. The red mark on the girl's face was all the evidence he needed. He restrained the French tutor from leaving.

"Hold her for Daniel," Giselle said in a controlled voice. She turned to Constance. "Let us wash your face with cool water."

The Legionnaire backed out of the room with the woman. He wanted so desperately just to strike the woman. Instead he roughly shoved her down on a nearby stool. Several others from the Royal Legion came into the room. "She struck the princess." The others stood glaring at the French woman.

"Is that how you treat your royalty at home?" One snarled at her, his face just inches from the frightened woman's face. The woman began to cry.

"Tears will get you nowhere with the Chancellor!" another threatened.

Another had gone to report the incident to Daniel who left what he was doing returned to his chambers. The first thing he saw was a woman cowed down on a stool encircled by five Legionnaires. The men parted when they became aware of Daniel in their midst.

The woman began to wail and to cry out. "Your majesty, please forgive me for this intrusion."

"Quiet!" Someone shouted.

Daniel was looking at the door to Constance's special chamber. It was still standing open. "Where is the princess?"

Giselle was still placing cool cloths on the girl's face. "Your Uncle Daniel is out there and wants you," she said to the girl whose own sobs were now reduced to intermittent gasps and hiccups.

"I can't go out there," Constance protested as she touched her still hurting face.

"You will if justice is to prevail." Giselle continued. "What you said and how you said it was not right.

"But she hit me," came the protest.

"After your words," Giselle answered.

"Constance, come here," Daniel's voice was heard through the open door.

"Let him see you," Giselle urged, "and answer him."

The girl went to the doorway but remained in the shadows of the room.

Daniel walked up to her and touched her swollen face. With his thumb, he gently wiped a tear from it.

"You struck the princess?" He had turned back to face the Mademoiselle. The French woman hung her head.

"Answer my question."

"Yes, Sire," she was barely audible.

"What did she do to you, did she hit you?"

The quiver in her voice made it difficult to understand her answer.

"I asked you, did she hit you?"

The woman shook her head not daring to look up.

Constance could feel the woman's terror. When Daniel turned again to her, she wondered if her fear was just like what the other person was feeling. "You did not hit her?" Daniel was asking Constance. "No, Sire," she replied grateful that she hadn't.

"Then, what did you do?"

She didn't want to tell Daniel that she had mocked her teacher. She knew that would be a punishable offense if someone had mocked her. She took a step backward into the shadows of the room. Daniel stepped through the doorway into the room with her.

"What did you do?" he asked again in a low voice.

"I mocked her," Constance said in a whisper. Daniel looked at Giselle who was standing a few feet away. She nodded.

"You received a just punishment."

Daniel returned to the outer chamber. No one moved wondering what had taken place within the girl's chambers in the soft quiet whispering that they could barely detect.

"Take her," he indicated the cowering woman, "Hold her in a cell." The woman let out with a wail. "Be quiet, woman, I am a just man." The woman was led away, still sobbing.

Daniel went back into the private rooms of the princess. He shut the door behind him and watched Giselle ministering a cooling salve to the face of the princess.

When they looked up at him, they saw tears in his eyes or maybe it was just the poor light. He turned and left without another word. Once in the throne room, he ordered the woman freed from the cell and to be told that her services were no longer needed in the castle.

The gossip that ran through the castle had the woman beheaded and the princess maimed. When the seamstress arrived, she did not know what to expect. Constance's docility was remarkable. There was little if any trace of the blow to her face. Rumors as usual were wrong.

The seamstress came armed with a pattern for riding pants. She muttered and fumed about ladies riding like men as she adapted the pants pattern to Constance's small size.

"Remember, she is a growing girl." Giselle said as she watched the woman attempt to make the pants for Constance.

"You should learn to ride like a woman," the seamstress growled as she fitted the pants on the princess.

"I know how." Constance replied. "I like to ride the spirited horses. You can't ride sidesaddle and stay on them."

"Remember," Giselle responded from across the room, "that is how you ended up spending so much time in this room."

The girl only nodded and got a pinch for wiggling at the wrong moment.

Secretly, Constance was excited. If Uncle Daniel was having 'proper 'riding pants made for her, was he going to let her ride his big horse again? Then she thought about how angry he had been with her that day several months ago. He had said she would never get up on that horse again. Maybe he had changed his mind.

When he arrived later that afternoon, she was surprised and a little apprehensive since he had been there in the morning. "Uncle Daniel," she recklessly approached him. "The seamstress is making 'riding pants' for me!" He nodded as she continued. "Does that mean I can go riding soon?"

Daniel looked at her earnest and innocent face. For a brief moment he wondered how such beauty could reside in the same person with the girl who deliberately provoked him or others with regularity. He marveled at the serenity of Giselle in spite of long weeks, days and hours cooped up with the princess. He reached out and gently touched the face that had worn such a red handprint just this morning.

Constance stood quivering when her Uncle touched her. It had been such a gentle touch.

"Discipline and pain," Daniel whispered just for her to hear. Her face reddened, not from a blow but from the awareness that she was beginning to understand.

"Maybe soon, we can go riding." If the truth would be known, he missed riding his horse.

"I have someone I want you to see."

"In the throne room?" she asked not really relishing having to put on one of her newly made royal gowns.

"No, in the garden. You are dressed for a walk in the garden, aren't you?"

She shrugged her shoulders. "I guess so. Are we going now?"

Daniel nodded. "Soon." He had sent Ian ahead of him to the area beside the garden. He wanted the two of them to see each other although he was not planning on introducing them to each other yet.

Ian had looked at the Chancellor's messenger in surprise. He had just finished a lesson in horsemanship when the messenger arrived. "Go to the far side of the royal gardens and wait."

He knew how to obey so he bowed in response to the messenger and started walking to the far side of the castle where the royal gardens were. He would then have to circumvent the large low walled garden to be in the far side. The words 'far side' seemed to mock him as his lesson in the area by the stables had been strenuous.

He could see no one in the gardens but there were privacy bushes at various points so someone could be watching to see if he obeyed. He selected a spot outside of the gardens from which he could see the gardens and waited.

A slight movement from behind some of the bushes indicated that there was someone watching. His legs were tired. He had been learning how to control his mount at the stables just by leg pressure. His slight built was a definite handicap on the big horse.

It seemed like he only looked away for a moment when he became aware of the Chancellor with a young lady at his side walking on the path of the garden. He watched them, as they seemed to be in a discussion. They came closer and closer to the wall that separated the gardens from where he was standing.

The girl was attractive. She must be the princess, he decided by her modest but stylish gown. She seemed to be interested in what the Chancellor was telling her. They stopped at a small bench and sat down. The Chancellor had chosen to sit looking toward the edge of the royal gardens.

"There is someone out there," Constance commented.

"Oh?" her uncle turned to look in the direction where she was pointing.

"Who do you suppose it is?" Constance asked in curiosity.

"Just a lad."

It was her turn to utter, "Oh."

"He looks like a fine lad," Uncle Daniel added.

"How can you tell from here?" Constance was puzzled by the positive response by her uncle.

"His clothes fit him well."

"Oh," Constance was still confused. "Giselle says clothes can deceive."

Her uncle laughed. "That is true. You thought I was a highwayman when I met you by my outer garments."

Constance blushed remembering when she discovered he was wearing light amour under his cloak and the crest of the kingdom. "But you were in hiding," she tried to excuse her blush.

"Your father wore well-fitting clothing." Daniel left the sentence unfinished.

She didn't have a response to this reference to her own father. She had known as most of the court knew that he was not what he pretended to be, the king. She hadn't thought much about him since her Uncle arrived. Even as a highwayman, her uncle wore his garments well.

She looked back out where the lad had been. He was talking with another lad who seemed dressed as a servant of the Chancellor.

"What are they talking about?" she asked.

"Ever curious, aren't you?" Daniel turned to her and smiled.

She was distracted by the kindness her uncle was showing her. When she looked again the two lads were walking away. Her face clouded over.

Daniel took her hand, and led her to other spots in the garden. "This is my favorite," he said sudden at a junction of paths that came from every direction meeting at a statue. "I used to dart down here and then choose another to go back on. It was my game of hide and seek."

"The statue!" Constance was standing still looking at it.

"A guardian angel," Daniel said. "Appropriate for this garden spot."

"She has wings."

Daniel nodded. "Don't ever try to climb up on her!" His voice was serious and firm.

Constance looked at him. She wanted to ask 'why' but his look told her that it was not a question to be asked.

"She is the Guardian Angel of our kingdom and all of those who are born into the royal family."

"Even me?" Constance said in awe.

"Yes, my dear princess, especially you."

Fascination

*I*an was running as fast as he could. He had about an hour of free time before he would be missed. Dodging merchant carts, food stalls, and animal dung, he made his way to the Church of St. Stephen that was wedged between a street market and the back wall of someone's villa.

He pulled open the massive door and stepped inside. The darkness of the inside of the church was frightening when the door closed behind him. It was several minutes before his eyes adjusted to the dim lighting. He dropped down on a bench in the back that was reserved for those in service to the royal household. The hard floor bit into his lean knees when he knelt. No one seemed to be inside the church. Did he dare go closer to the altar? He really wanted to look at the massive cross that hung behind the tabernacle. Would God strike him dead if he went closer?

His decision was made for him. "What are you doing here, lad?" A shrouded figure spoke to him out of the shadows.

"The priest?" he asked with a trembling voice.

"I am," answered the figure as he drew nearer. "You are in the king's service?"

Ian nodded. "Yes, Father."

"Are you in trouble?"

He remained mute not knowing how to answer that question.

"Answer me, lad." The priest was now upon him.

"I", Ian stuttered before pulling the crucifix out from his shirt. "Tell me about this," he said.

The priest demanded, "Where did you get it? Did you steal it?"

"Oh, no, Father, my friend gave it to me."

The priest reached for the crucifix on the cord around Ian's neck. "It was mine," the priest said. "I gave it to another in service to the king."

Ian whispered, "Kait?"

"What about Kait, is he in trouble?"

"I do not know. He gave me this one night. I have not seen him since."

"What did he say when he gave it to you?"

"That he was a believer too, and that I was to keep this. It is getting late Father; I need to get back to the castle." Ian was now standing and glancing at the doorway.

"Bless you my son, and come again." The priest placed the crucifix on the cord back around Ian's neck. "I shall be watching for you." Ian made the sign of the cross before darting toward the door. He would have to hurry to get back.

His feet flew like they had wings and he had been in his room only a few moments before the Chancellor sent for him. As he straightened his garments and made an attempt to smooth his hair, he forgot about the cord that showed at the neck of his tunic.

The Chancellor was pacing the floor when Ian arrived. "You are slow, lad."

"Sire," Ian bowed and waited. The crucifix had slipped out of his tunic in his bow.

The Chancellor seemed to staring at something on him. Ian only had a moment before the Chancellor reacted.

"What is this?" The Chancellor had in his hand the crucifix and was putting pressure on the cord that was still around Ian's neck.

Ian was silent. He did not know how to explain the crucifix nor did he know if wearing it was going to cause him a great deal of pain in discipline. He stood trembling and waiting.

"You do not know what you are wearing?" the Chancellor asked. "Who gave it to you? A priest?"

Ian saw a light of escape as the Chancellor had asked about a priest. The priest had placed it back on Ian's neck. "Yes, a priest."

"Are you a believer?"

"Yes, Sire," he trembled at his admission.

"Why?" The Chancellor had released his hold on the crucifix so that it dropped back down inside Ian's tunic.

The lad had no ready answer.

"You are wearing the reason," the Chancellor looked across the room.

Ian followed his glance. The Royal Crest hung on the far wall. He had never noticed the crucifix image in one of the sections before. An involuntary 'oh' came out of his mouth.

"You saw her?" Looking back at the lad, he changed the direction in the conversation.

"Yes, Sire."

"Good, she noticed you."

Ian felt his face redden.

"Does that embarrass you?"

He did not know how to answer the king.

"She is eager to see you again," the Chancellor laughed as though that was a private joke.

"Soon, Sire?" the lad asked.

"No." He watched the lad's countenance carefully. There was neither a flicker of disappointment nor of relief. Obviously, the lad was not expecting much either way.

"Would you like to see her again?"

"As you wish, Sire," was the proper answer expected from any of the servants to such a question.

"Take care of your soul," the Chancellor concluded the meeting and sent Ian back to his room.

Ian stared out the window toward where the steeple of St. Stephen's rose in the dark night. The word 'soul' drifted around in his mind not allowing him rest. Tightly, he held the crucifix in his hand, letting its sharp edges cause him pain and he prayed.

The next weeks were a jumble of lessons and diligent work. Constance was so busy that she forgot to complain or plan any mischief. This was a great relief to Giselle as she followed her charge from lesson to lesson with little interruption. Art and music were the highlights for Constance's days since she enjoyed listening to music or learning to play one of several instruments. In art, she enjoyed the imagery of a painting where her imagination always wanted to put her into the scene. Portraits were boring. Statues intrigued her and as often as she could request it, she spent time in the royal gardens enjoying the varied statues, some of which embarrassed her in their nudity. Her favorite was the Angel that Uncle Daniel had first shown her.

Ian was on a similar course of study that included hours in horsemanship. Some days left him so tired that he nearly fell asleep when he was in the common dining hall with the other servants. They teased him one night after he totally missed one of the dishes being passed around. Fortunately, it was nearly empty when it slipped through his fingers. Ralle was immediately alert. The session with the master of the Chancellor's servants was painful but short. Not being allowed to finish his meal had been more stressful. A couple of the other lads slipped him some of the hard biscuits to satiate his hunger after he returned to his room.

There was no time to slip off to the church. Ian wanted to know more about the God who was on the crest of the King. It was not a question he could ask his tutors or even the other boys. He hit upon a plan. Waking up early while it was still dark, he slipped out of the castle and ran to St. Stephen's. He found a priest there praying at the altar and doing ritualistic moves. This intrigued him more. He returned to the castle just in time to eat standing up in the corner of the servant's kitchen before going to the stables for his early morning lesson in horsemanship.

Day after day, this predawn run to the church went undetected until on his trip back to the castle one morning, he passed an open window just as a woman threw out a bucket of waste to the pigs. It covered him nearly from head to toe. He stank! He detoured to his turret room leaving behind a path of evidence. How was he going to get the smell and stuff off him? He had another change of clothing, but it was dressier and reserved for appearances in the court.

It had not taken Ralle long to figure out that something was amiss as he followed his nose and the trail of water and slop to Ian's room. Although he was master of those who served in the royal chamber, he had been warned to not treat the lad too severely by the Chancellor himself. He opened the door to Ian's room and gasped as the putrid scent rushed out.

When the door opened unannounced, Ian frozen with terror. He saw that it was Ralle. There was nothing to do but wait for the inevitable beating that he would receive from the servant master. Ralle's face was almost purple from rage. "Where have you been?"

Ian was so frightened that he could not speak.

"Your clothing is ruined!" Ian dropped his eyes and waited. "Take your clothes off." Ralle grabbed the water urn and doused Ian and most of the room with the water in it.

Ian tried to hide the crucifix as his clothing was ripped off of him. "What is that?" Ralle snatched it from the boy's hand and threw it into the pile of putrid clothing. Ian's sleeping blanket was tossed at him. "Wrap yourself in that!" Ralle kicked the smelly pile of clothing into a corner of the room. "Come with me," he ordered.

Dressed only in his scant blanket, Ian obediently followed Ralle down the hall and into another hallway that he thought looked familiar. A Legionnaire stood guard outside the door where Ralle knocked. Ian avoided looking at the guard but he knew the man could smell him. A few words were spoken when the door was opened and then Ian was thrust into the next room.

The Chancellor, in a partial state of getting dressed looked at Ian in amusement. "Bad morning?" Ian did not answer. The Chancellor waved Ralle out of his chambers as he considered what to do. It was obvious that the boy was mortified and very frightened. "Where are your clothes?"

Ian attempted a bow without showing any more of his bare skin. "Sire, I went to St. Stephen's before dawn. The priest is teaching me about the crucifix."

"Your clothes?" the question was asked again.

"In my room." Ian replied.

"The crucifix?"

Ian reached for it and then remembered. "Ralle tossed it with my clothes."

The Chancellor rang for his attendants and gave instructions to clean the lad and to the other to go fetch his soiled clothing and the crucifix.

After a thorough scrubbing in a tub, Ian was given clean clothing and the cleaned crucifix. The Chancellor left instructions that Ian was to be fed and to remain in the King's private rooms.

Ian spent the time on his knees praying. When the Chancellor returned, he found the lad still on his knees but asleep. Upon awakening, Ian scrambled to his feet and bowed, "Forgive me, Sire."

The laugh that came out of the Chancellor's mouth disturbed Ian. "For sleeping or for praying?"

Ian blushed.

"I need to add a new subject to your studies, I see."

Ian trembled wondering how he was going to add anything more to his already packed day.

"The first thing every morning, you will go to St. Stephen's and study with the priest. He will instruct you in the Church and in other subjects as well. You will begin tomorrow morning." Stunned, Ian bowed.

"The seamstress will be making you some additional clothing. What you wore today is not suitable."

"The blanket?" the lad whispered.

"No, the smelly clothing, I had them destroyed."

"Sire?

"Your room has been cleaned. Go to it and rest. Tomorrow will begin your new schedule."

Ian bowed and followed servant that led him back to his room. It was spotless with not a trace of the putrid smell lingering in the air. His straw mattress was now on a frame raised above the floor with a new blanket. Ian knelt at the window where he could see the church spires and wept.

Faith Developed

*I*an enjoyed his new schooling. He arrived each morning before the Mass and then sat at the Father's feet, learning about the crucifix. He had been baptized as a child. Now he was learning about how a person grows in the faith. Each day he was turned out from the building while the believers finished the Mass so the mystery of the Eucharist was denied him. Afterward he was invited to return for lessons as his curiosity and questions grew.

"Be patient, my son," the priest would say when he asked questions. One morning the priest was called away for an emergency in the middle of the lesson. Remaining behind in the church, alone in the silence and its magnificence, Ian felt drawn to the large crucifix that hung on the wall behind the tabernacle. The larger than human sized figure seemed to be beckoning him. Slowly, he approached the altar area. Father had taken him close before, but with admonition of not touching anything. He glanced over his shoulder and saw no one in the rest of the church. Surely, now was the time to touch it, he thought to himself.

Cautiously, he crept nearer to the altar. He could not reach the carved figure from where he stood. He put his foot on the ornate stone trim of the altar and pulled himself up. He touched the feet of the carved figure.

"What are you doing?" A man's voice resounded from the darken interior of the church. Frightened, Ian fell backward and down off his precarious perch at the altar. He could hear the removal of a sword from the scabbard. A Legionnaire came out of the darkness of the back of the church.

Ian knelt in submission for the expected sword thrust. "Sire," the boy whimpered.

The Legionnaire was now standing over him, surprised to recognize the favored young servant of his King. He replaced the sword and knelt down by the young man. "Why dare you blaspheme our Lord and God?"

Ian whimpered awaiting his death by the sword. The hand that raised his bowed head was firm but gentle. "Lad." Again, the Legionnaire spoke.

Opening his eyes, he looked into the face of the Legionnaire who had been guarding the door the day he had been so disgracefully marched to the King's chamber smelling of the hog slop. "I slipped, I only wanted to get nearer the cross."

"You surely did that." the man holding his chin firmly in his hand. "But you did not slip, that is a lie."

Ian tried to pull his head from the viselike grip of the Legionnaire. "I am sorry," he said softly.

"Has the priest taught you about lying?" The grip on his chin did not lessen.

"Yes, Sire," Ian answered.

"Come," he tugged at the boy. "We both will be in trouble if the priest finds us here at the altar."

Ian yielded readily as the Legionnaire guided him back to the bench reserved in the back of the church for those in service to the royal household.

"You must go to confession for your deed and lie." the man knelling beside him at the back said. "Do you understand?"

"Then he will know what I did," whispered Ian.

"Precisely," answered the Legionnaire.

"He will kill me," Ian's voice trembled.

"No, my lad, he will forgive you. He is Christ when you confess to him."

The trembling of the young man was great.

"What he will do is scold you, and forgive you when you repent. Do you know that word?"

"Repent?"

"Yes, something that Princess Constance doesn't seem to understand yet."

Ian looked boldly into the Legionnaire's face. *How dare he speak of the Princess at a time like this!*

"Your lesson today is repentance. When you turn away from your misdeed in sorrow and shame, tell it to the priest, ask for forgiveness, receive your penance, and the prayer of absolution, it will be as though you did not do what you did. God forgives you."

Ian nodded as he remembered the priest telling him those things at one time. "How do you know so much?"

The Legionnaire cuffed him lightly on the side of the head. "Inquisitive, aren't you?"

"Sorry, Sire," the lad ducked his head.

"Wait for his return and then confess to him." The words were firm.

"What if he does not come back soon?"

"Then they will deal with your late return to the castle when you get there." The Legionnaire stood and left the church.

Ian alternated between crying and fear until the priest returned. He did exactly as the Legionnaire told him. The priest, although perturbed by the boy's misdeed, responded just as the man had said he would.

A chastened young man returned in time for his horsemanship lesson at the stable. No one seemed to notice his late return but he was sure he would hear about it sometime before nightfall.

"The Chancellor wants you," the young man from the King's private chambers said to him after the evening meal.

Ian turned from his path toward his room to follow the servant to the Chancellor's chambers. Fear haunted him the whole way.

The room was empty when he arrived so he stood quietly waiting. His eyes came to rest on the royal crest. He still did not fully understand the meaning of the crucifix but he knew more than he had known the last time he had been in that room.

"What have you learned today," the King's voice from behind him startled him.

"Not to lie. Ian blurted out unexpectedly.

"To me?"

"No, Sire," he had turned to the speaking voice and bowed.

"I mean," he tried to amend his statement.

The raised hand stopped him. "I know what you meant. Whom did you lie to."?

"A Legionnaire."

"And he whipped you for it?" the King was playing with Ian's emotions.

"No, Sire."

"Why not?" The question came thundering out.

"He taught me how to repent."

"That is the priest's job."

"But I did not lie to the priest," Ian was confused by the direction of the conversation.

"It is a wonder he did not take his sword to you," the Chancellor was enjoying the discomfort of the lad.

Ian shuddered as he remembered thinking that very thing when he had been found at the altar. "He thought of it, Sire."

"How do you know?"

"He unsheathed his sword." The lad was staring at a spot just over the King's shoulder as he remembered the sound.

"What had you done to deserve that kind of action?"

Ian's eyes came back to his King's. "I beg your forgiveness, Sire." He bowed and continued. "I".

"Don't tell me," the Chancellor stopped him. "I already know." After what seemed a long time, he continued. "Did you make confession to the priest."

Ian's face reddened. "Yes, Sire."

"You are dismissed," the King said softly.

Daniel paced the floor of the main room of his private chamber tossing around the information he had been told by the Legionnaire and the lad. He wondered how he would have handled that same event if it had been Constance. He felt himself shudder thinking of having to deal with such a thing with her. *She probably would have been defiant!*

It seemed like it had been a long time since Uncle Daniel had visited with her. Constance was eager to show him some of the paintings she had done. The tutor had told her that she was doing very well. Really what she wanted was to go to the Royal Gardens in hope of seeing the young man who been loitering outside the garden wall. She was aware that her uncle was preparing someone to be her companion, whatever that meant, and wondered if the young man she had seen was he.

She asked Giselle for the hundredth time, "Did the courier give my message to my uncle?"

Giselle laughed. "You would think that your message was the most important thing in the kingdom today."

Constance all but stomped her foot in her exasperation. "Quit laughing at me!"

"It is more that I am laughing at a young child who is not as old as you."

Constance was fidgeting with the bow on her dress. "I am too big for bows," she replied.

"Yes, definitely a young child still."

"I am not!"

Giselle looked up at the girl. "And I had thought you were growing up. Getting bigger, you are. Have you forgotten that you are to become more mature as you get bigger?"

Constance stomped off to the other room.

"And don't plan anything to get his attention," Giselle called after her. She knew her charge well.

"What does he expect of me being all cooped up here in these rooms? Why can't I go back to my own rooms?"

Daniel had quietly entered the outer room. Giselle started to stand. He shook his head and put his finger to his lip. "Let her talk," he whispered. "She obviously has a complaint."

Giselle shook her head 'no' to the idea of complaint.

Constance had noticed the non-response from her lady. "Where are my riding clothes?"

"You are not scheduled for riding. They are put up," Giselle answered standing in the doorway between the two rooms. "You have a visitor."

Constance had torn the offending bow from her dress. "It fell off. The seamstress did not do a good job!" She had missed Giselle's last statement totally.

"Constance, your uncle is in the other room." Giselle responded.

"You are lying to me," Constance accused.

Daniel restrained himself from saying anything. *It seems that lying is the topic today,* he thought.

Giselle, torn between wanting to say more but her knowledge of Daniel's presence in the next room left her silent. She backed out of the inner room and turned to face Daniel. Her eyes glistened with tears.

"I did not say you could leave," Constance called out to her. Daniel pointed to the other door. Giselle nodded and left. Constance stomped into the room halting suddenly. "Oh!" she gasped as he closed the distance between then in two steps. "No!" she tried to cry out as he grasped her tightly and pinched her on her backside.

As she struggled to get away from his grip, he continued to subject her to repeated punishing pinches. Each one seemed to be harder and longer than the one before. When she cried out, he placed his hand over her mouth and hissed "discipline and pain."

Tears ran down her cheeks when she finally nodded. He hoped her nod meant that she understood. He released his grip both on her body and her mouth. She stood shaking in pain and rage. "How dare you," she spat at him.

Daniel felt anger not as great as when she had nearly killed his horse, but still beyond anything he preferred to feel. "Get out of that dress you mutilated!"

"Why?" she dared to reply.

The seamstress had left the measuring stick in the princess's chambers. Daniel grabbed it and pushed her into the inner room. He thrust a dressing gown at her. "Put this on."

The fear that she had when he had beaten her in the woods was now real as she looked at her uncle holding the stick. She did what he said, attempting to cover her modesty as she put on the dressing gown and pulled off the dress simultaneously. When the offending dress was free, Daniel threw it across the room before he took the stick to her legs and backside.

Constance cried out and found his hand again covering her mouth. She ceased to struggle as the blows continued.

The stick broke. Daniel dropped the short piece from his hand and pulled Constance to him as Constance continued to cry. He looked at his handprint still visible where he had covered her mouth and turned his head away in sorrow. When she had quieted, he tucked her into bed. Picking up the broken stick pieces, he left.

Outside the chambers, Giselle was seated on a low stool, weeping into her skirts. The Legionnaire watched the old woman and wondered what was taking place inside the rooms.

The door opened suddenly. Both Giselle and the Legionnaire had no warning before their King was before them. He thrust the broken stick into the Legionnaire's hand before he turned to Giselle. "She needs you."

Thinking about it later, neither Giselle nor the Legionnaire could remove from their memories the tears in Daniel's eyes.

Daniel stumbled into his own private rooms, and with a hand gesture, sent his personal servants away. For a long time, he knelt in front of the Royal Crest remembering the past, both the just happened past and the night his wife had died in his arms. Constance had not even been weaned, and her mother had died that same night. He had to flee for his life as his younger brother not only usurped the throne within hours after their deaths but also accused Daniel of killing the women. It was an ugly inheritance for the now future queen. He cried in private although his most faithful servants knew of his grieving agony as he remained on his knees before the Royal Crest.

Late, in the dark night, the priest at St. Stephen's awakened to the urgent request to come to the castle. Fearful, the old man was afraid that more tragedy had befallen the royal family. He remembered the dark night of the multiple deaths when the baby princess was left without a mother. He prayed the *Kryie Eleison* as he hurried along behind the Legionnaire who had come for him. Another Legionnaire behind them carried the chrism oil. The priest himself carried a host in a small leather pouch.

In Daniel's private chambers he found the anxious servants. He was escorted into the room where Daniel was still kneeling.

"Bless you, Chancellor Daniel," the priest said softly.

The two men, one of royal blood, and the other the servant of the Most Holy God, talked until sunrise. At dawn, the priest heard the king's confession ending with absolution.

Then he went to the Princess's chamber where he found her resting in the comfortable care of Giselle. The Priest spent some time explaining to the young woman about her responsibilities not only to the kingdom but foremost to God. She had been taught but never was receptive. This morning, she listened with respect, something the priest had not seen in her before. He prayed for her, and asked her to consider adding time at the Church as part of her daily life.

"There is a chapel here," she exclaimed.

"It has been unused for years," the priest answered.

"Why?" the question came out so innocently.

"Your father decided he didn't need it."

Constance looked up into the face of the priest and saw tears.

"Oh."

"Come to the church, St. Stephen's," he gently requested again.

Her countenance was sober and reflective. She nodded.

He blessed her and anointed her for healing.

She was embarrassed that he knew about her wounds of the night before.

"When you have learned more about your faith and the Church, you will understand."

He blessed Giselle and left.

The Hair Pin

The trips to St. Stephen's were exciting for Constance. Although she had run away from the castle many times in the past, she had never gone directly into the city preferring the forests and fields as her places of escape. Two Legionnaires accompanied her each time she left the castle. The priest was delighted that she had responded to his invitation. Now he had two young people to teach. Sometimes Ian was still there when she went. They avoided looking at each other, he because of his position and she because of a shyness that was new to her personality. Giselle sometimes accompanied her with the Legionnaires and noted this new shyness. She smiled to herself and praise God for the maturing of her charge.

Constance knew only the bare rudiments of her faith. The priest was not surprise. He started with the basic prayers and the Ten Commandments. Just as the lad, to his joy, she was a quick learner.

She had many questions about what she was seeing as they traversed the city daily. Constance saw people doing things she could not have imagined. When they passed close to the area where Ian had been drenched with hog slop, she paused to stare at the crude small huts and muddy plots that surrounded them. Giselle was at a loss to explain the poverty that Constance saw.

"Why do they live that way?" she asked her constant companions.

"It is where they were born. Their families have always lived there."

"Those big animals that stand in the mud and make odd sounds?"

"Pigs," snorted one of the Legionnaires.

The first morning she noticed that St. Stephen's was not the big church where she had attended her father's funeral. The priest patiently explained that St. Stephen's was more the ordinary peasant's church. She puzzled over that for several days. "Peasant's church?" she asked. "There is another church?"

Father nodded. "Where the Royalty worships, Blessed Be Our God Cathedral." He paused and wondered how he was going to explain why she was studying at St. Stephen's.

Constance was silent pondering the information. Father had left off in the middle of asking for her recitation of the prayers he had been teaching her. She looked up at him. "Did my Uncle Daniel study here?"

The priest looked at her. Her expression was innocent. "He was taught at the other one."

"Why?"

"Your prayers," he retorted.

For a moment, there was a flicker of anger in her eyes for his refusal to answer her question. Then she began to recite the ones she knew well, stumbling only when she got to the Creed.

"Today's lesson is on the Ten Commandments." Father said after he corrected her error in the Creed." For the rest of time that day he drilled her in reciting those in correct order.

"What do they mean?" she asked although she understood 'do not kill and do not steal'.

"That is tomorrow's lesson," he closed the session with the sign of the cross and prayer.

Constance lingered by one of the shops where a shoemaker worked. "I want to see inside," she told the Legionnaire.

The 'no' annoyed her.

"Why not? I am the princess!"

The two men looked at each other. "Daniel would not like it if he heard you say that."

"That I am the princess?" She stood with her feet firmly planted in front of the shop.

The one Legionnaire shook his head. "What did he tell you?"

Constance thought for a moment before she yielded to the fact that the two men would not allow her to go into the shop. She could hear her uncle's voice giving instructions to her before he had let her go even the first time to St. Stephen's. *Obey their every command.* She remembered well the look he had given her. His most recent discipline of her was still very fresh in her memory

A few days later, Daniel decided to visit Constance while one of her tutors was with her in her chambers. He had been disturbed when the Legionnaire's had reported her desire to go into the shops along their route back and forth to St. Stephen's. The art tutor was watching her paint, mostly using his pointer to indicate where she should concentrate on her painting next.

Tense from Daniel's presence, Constance dropped her paint-laden brush. Her tutor insisted that she clean up her mess before continuing her painting. Embarrassed, she obeyed while Daniel watched her get down on her knees to scrape and wipe the paint from the stone floor. The tutor left after the brush was properly cleansed.

"Would you like to walk in the Royal Garden's?" Daniel asked. never been in before, Daniel was showing her some new statues and work being done outside the Throne Room in readiness for some expected visitors from a kingdom to the south. Constance insisted that he take her to the Angel statue.

"You are being demanding," Daniel observed to her.

"Who cares about visitors from the south," Constance answered.

He stopped walking so suddenly that she ran into him. "Oh!" she uttered in surprise at the stinging pinch.

Then ignoring her negative sentence, he continued. "They are coming by boat."

Her curiosity was raised. "Can I go down and see the boat?"

"The harbor is too dangerous for you."

"Why?" She had placed some distance between herself and Daniel.

"There are too many people and things down there that you do not understand. There are people that could hurt you."

"Send me with the Legionnaires," she offered coquettishly.

"No."

"Why?"

Daniel pointed to a nearby bench. "Sit down and I will try to explain it to you."

There was a moment of tenseness before Constance sat.

"You are curious about everything. You still argue with whomever I entrust your care to including myself."

Constance's pout seemed to increase with each word he spoke.

"That look will get you nowhere, including not being present in the Throne Room to meet the visitors."

She jumped up to her feet intent on disputing her uncle. He took one step toward her and she retreated to her seat. "Why must I be presented in the Throne Room?"

"That is the way it is done. You are the future queen and most visitors like to go home saying they met you. Sometimes I wonder why."

Constance was swinging her legs in agitation and boredom. "Uncle Daniel," she spoke with an earnest inflection of voice.

"Why can't I go to the harbor to see the boat? That is what I would do. Meet the boat and them they would invite me on board to show me the grandness of their ship."

"Maybe their ship is not grand but a working vessel that usually catches fish. It might actually stink." Daniel was playing right back to her imagination.

"Then I would hold my nose," she retorted.

"The answer is still 'no'," Daniel smiled at the thought of the royal visitors coming on a fishing vessel.

Constance had turned her eyes away. "Where is the boy?"

"I imagine he is busy,"

"Oh," Constance stood up. "I want to see the Angel statue now!"

Her uncle looked at her. "No, our time is finished in the gardens for today. I must prepare for the visitors."

Constance was ahead of him on the path. If he was not going to take her to the Angel statue, she was going to be independent and walk ahead of him alone.

He let her. Once back inside the castle, he sent her back to his chambers with a Legionnaire. She was irritated when the man offered her his arm as he escorted her back to her rooms. When she ignored his courtesy, he growled and said, "If you refuse to used my arm, I may find it necessary to take hold of yours."

She glanced at the Legionnaire and recalled that he was often her guide to St. Stephen's. He could be very menacing. She wondered if her uncle Daniel knew how menacing this man was. She sighed under her breath, and reached her hand to his extended arm to accept his escort.

Daniel had stopped in a doorway and watched the reluctant obedience of his niece. 'Lord,' he sighed to himself.

Two hours later, her presence was desired in the Throne Room. She went, dressed properly by Giselle. When she had fussed at the dress selection, Giselle only commented, "There are no bows on this one."

The same Legionnaire was sent to take her to the Throne Room. His glowering glance kept Constance silent about accepting his arm as he escorted her.

Her full name was announced just as she entered the room. Daniel met her a few feet in and took her to the visitors who were standing off to one side. The court had grown surprisingly quiet with such a formal entrance by Constance. She curtsied to Daniel and again to the visitors. "My niece and future queen," Daniel said to those waiting to meet her.

"How lovely you are my dear," an elderly woman spoke when Constance offered her hand after her bow. She only heard the visitors as they spoke to her as she kept her eyes downcast. She didn't want to see these strangers who had come by the ship that Daniel would not allow her to visit.

"My niece," he repeated with each out stretched hand. Constance endured the sometimes limp and occasionally firm handshakes. She was doing only what he asked and nothing more.

"Your second cousin, Lady Rachel," the change in words startled Constance and she looked up to see a pleasant woman, about Uncle Daniel's age.

"She is becoming quite the young lady," the woman said warmly. "My dear, I am so glad to meet you."

Constance was in a quandary. She realized she needed to respond but she didn't know how. She murmured, "Thank you," and hoped that her uncle would be satisfied.

After a couple more people, she had met all the guests. "You are excused," Daniel spoke to her quietly as he signaled for the Legionnaire to escort her.

"She handles herself well, doesn't she," one of the visitors commented as they were escorted to the banquet hall.

Daniel stood at the head of the table and bowed his head. Those who were Christian believers also bowed while Daniel asked a blessing on the meal. "Such a man of faith," another one of the visitor's seated close to Daniel commented. "Is that how you got the throne back?"

Daniel laughed. "God blessed me with a gift that helped me. I was never on the throne. My brother took it, and I did not challenge him for he had also accused me of murder."

The group nodded. They had all heard the tale but never from the one who had been banished. They were eager to hear his side, since he was now King after his brother's sudden death.

"The people are happy with me," Daniel didn't finish the story much to the collective disappointment of his guests. "Constance will be Queen when she is of age." He commenced to eat. Small talk between dinner partners carefully avoided speculation.

The Throne Room had been transformed into a Ballroom by the time the meal was complete. After an appropriate time, all invited guests and visitors made their way into the transformed room. The Throne at one end and the Royal Crest hanging at the other were the only objects that indicated the true use of the room. An orchestra was playing and soon many were dancing to the various traditional dances of the Kingdom.

Upstairs in Constance's rooms, she could hear the music and occasional laughter. She was restless. Then, she got an idea. Giselle had reminded her of the solemn exhortation by Daniel to her and those who were responsible for her. He had said they were to keep charge of her and their very lives would be at stake if she disappeared.

Giselle was almost as good a seamstress as the one who made all of the dresses for Constance. Seated by the window and listening to the music from the Throne Room, she embroidered delicate flowers on the collar of one of Constance's new gowns. The Legionnaires were listening to the music, sometimes humming along and enjoying the peaceful evening.

Constance slipped outside on the stone balcony. If anyone questioned her, she would say it was to hear the music more clearly. When no one noticed, she sat up on the stonewall and studied the stones that made up the outside of the castle. She had noticed before there seemed to be a pattern that almost resembled steps going downward from the balcony. It was twilight when she lifted one foot over and then the other, and descended down the wall clinging to those stones that did protrude like hidden steps. In the last few feet, the stones had with fewer footholds so she dropped down to the ground with a light thud behind some bushes. She tore her dress in two places by the time she untangled herself from the bushes. There was no alarm or outcry from the rooms above her.

It took her a few minutes to find an entrance to the Royal Gardens. It was a gardener's gate, which swung open with a squeak. She hid herself under some low trees and waited to see if anyone had heard the gate.

It was easy to find her way to where the Throne Room opened out into the garden just by listening to the music and laughter. Finally, in the shadow of a cluster of statues, ringed with trimmed bushes, Constance sat down to watch the festivities inside.

Upstairs, the Legionnaires and Giselle were frantic. Giselle noticed that she had not seen nor heard the princess for a while and went into the inner room. Her scream brought the men on the run.

"Have you seen the girl?" the frantic woman cried out.

"Did she go out on the balcony?" one man asked.

They all looked at each other. One grinned in spite of his fears of Daniel's wrath for letting her get away from them. "Do we sound an alarm?"

"No, that would disturb the festivities in the Throne Room!"

"If we can find her without letting know that she was gone . . ."

"We will still have to tell him," another interrupted. The third man was staring down at the bushes below the balcony. They seemed to be damaged. He thought he could see something caught on them.

"She left this way!"

"How do you know?" Giselle asked. She was wringing her hands.

The Legionnaire climbed over the low wall and without too much difficulty made his way down the exterior of the stone castle. He noted the broken branches and pulled two small pieces of cloth off the bushes. The other two men followed him down and examined the small torn pieces. "Looks like her dress," one stated.

"Oh, please find her," Giselle called down. She returned to the interior and wept. "Oh child, you do not know what you have done," she wailed.

The three men were not men of fear but each was aware of the way Daniel had instructed them. They began to search the area. "The gate is open," one whispered when they came to the gardener's gate. Laughter came from the far side of the garden that faced the Throne Room.

"She is probably over there," another replied also in a whisper. They each nodded in agreement. Stealthily they crept across the garden avoiding the graveled paths where any sound of their footsteps might give them away. They spied her sitting among the statues.

"She will scream if we sneak up on her."

"Not if I can help it," another one whispered.

They planned their moves all the while watching the princess some distance away. "What if she runs?"

"Then they will all know inside," the one who had first climbed down the wall answered.

"She can't hide with the light-colored gown on." The men nodded in unison.

In solidarity, the three began to creep up upon where Constance was sitting. She moved and changed her position. They held their breaths until she had made herself more comfortable. In unison they moved forward, one on each flank and one directly behind where she was sitting.

She saw her Uncle Daniel dancing with a woman. She saw him speaking into the woman's ear and then they both laughed. She experienced. a new emotion for her. Jealousy! She desired to see more of the activities inside and unaware of anything in the gardens. A hand over her mouth stifled her scream as she was roughly hauled from her hiding place. The three men lifted her feet off the ground and carried her away from the open doors of the Throne Room. She struggled as they held her tighter to the point that she was in pain. They took her back through the gardener's gate and around behind the stables before they set her back on the ground.

"Listen carefully," said the man who still had his hand over her mouth. "You have caused us great grief tonight. If you weren't the princess, we would beat you severely."

"We will leave that to your uncle," another one added. The men nodded.

Constance's initial fear only grew larger. If the Legionnaires encouraged Daniel. She fainted.

"Well, that solves getting her back to her room quietly." one commented.

"Make sure she isn't faking."

"She isn't, let's get her up to her room quickly. Giselle will work with her faint."

In the Throne Room, Daniel received the information of Constance's escapade while dancing with his cousin, Rachel. "Would you like to spend some time with the young princess," he asked her. He wanted to see his cousin's reaction to the girl when the girl was not on display.

"Certainly," Rachel smiled. "Let me inform Felix."

"Would you husband want to come also?"

"No," Rachel laughed. "We just keep each other informed especially on trips outside of the kingdom. Security, you know."

Daniel did know which is why he had refused Constance's request to go down to the harbor.

On the way to his private chambers, he shared with Rachel about Constance's difficulty in learning to obey and what the message from the Legionnaire's had said about finding her in the garden watching the festivities.

Rachel mused as they entered Daniel's private rooms, "Maybe she needs to be trusted more."

That got a short laugh from Daniel. "Maybe is the right word but for her it means her way, not the obedient way."

Constance woke on her own bed. For a brief moment, she forgot what had gone on. "Where is my gown?"

"The one you tore?" Giselle grumbled. "It will take me many hours to repair what you did to it."

"How did I get here?"

"They brought you," Giselle pointed at the three Legionnaires standing in the doorway.

A disturbance in the outer room interrupted anything more Giselle or the Legionnaires might have said to her. A courier announced that Chancellor Daniel and his cousin were on their way up to visit with the princess.

Snatching another gown from the growing collection that the

dressmaker had made, Giselle waved the men out. "Put it on, and hurry. Your hair is a mess!" Giselle had the young princess ready in record time. "If you Uncle finds out what you have done," Giselle threatened Constance.

"The Chancellor requests the Princess Constance's presence in his greeting room," another courier announced.

Escorted by two of the three Legionnaires, Constance made her entrance within a few minutes. Other than being a little flushed from the rush of dressing in a hurry, she seemed normal.

Rachel began the conversation. Soon the two cousins were chatting away, starting with things that girls like and moving on into the most current event. Constance glanced quickly at her uncle when Rachel brought up that he had told her that she had been watching from the Royal Gardens.

"You wouldn't like being down there much except maybe for the fine music being played. Most of us adults fake our happiness when we would rather just be watching and listening."

"You are bored with that stuff?'" Constance was amazed. "What about when he," her eyes glanced at her uncle, "was whispering in your ear and you both laughed?"

"I will tell you a little secret. We were laughing about how someone else was dancing, or maybe clutching his partner because he doesn't dance well at all."

"Oh."

"You are beautiful, Constance. You are bold, something you must learn to control and you also have intelligence. What wonderful gifts God has bestowed. The two women were seated on a settee at one end of the room. Daniel had removed himself to the far end.

"Did you really come on a boat?" Constance blurted out.

"Yes, it is easier than riding in a coach over the lands between here and where I now live."

"Uncle Daniel won't let me go down to the harbor to see it."

"He is a very wise man, Constance. There are dangers at the harbor, and even more dangers if you have beauty and daring." the other woman told the younger girl. She noticed the beginning of a pout on the young girl's face.

Rachel smiled. "You thought he was being mean, didn't you?"

Constance nodded. "I want to see your ship. All I can see from here are the tops of some of the masts and the sparkling water beyond."

Rachel was stroking the girl. She reached up to her own hair that sparkled from the light shining off diamond-studded hairpins. She pulled out one of the pins and set it into Constance's hair. "My gift to you. Maybe Cousin Daniel will see that you get some more."

The young girl looked at her uncle standing at the other end.

Daniel nodded. "Yes, it is time you begin to show your royalty."

Constance looked back at Rachel before she again asked her uncle. "When can I see her boat?"

Daniel almost laughed for she was so consistently stubborn about what she really wanted.

Rachel answered. "Maybe the next time I come." She knew that would be several years and by that time the young girl would be bursting into mature womanhood.

Constance fully expected her uncle to deal with her behavior after the visitors left. When he didn't send for her or come to her rooms, she was mystified. Daily, she went to St. Stephen's protected by three very fierce looking Legionnaires. They rarely spoke to her. She caused them no problems. Knowing her reputation, they were mystified.

The priest found her more receptive to his instructions as she began to ask questions. "Confession is a sacrament, one of seven," he had just finished saying when she interrupted him.

"Seven confessions?" she said.

Father tapped his foot that he did when he was annoyed with her. "Holy Sacraments," he stated clearly.

Constance bowed her head in acknowledgement of the sharp correction.

"Confession is what God requires of you when you have sinned, like being disobedient or talking back." Father was angry for her frivolous comment that showed in the exacting way he was pronouncing his words to her. "Something you have yet to do," he added.

The next hour was spent in detailed instruction for confession the next time she came to St. Stephen's. "It will be the first thing you will do!"

Constance felt her ears reddening. She wondered but did not say aloud, *and what if I don't come.* She knew that the Legionnaires would make sure she came. She felt a shudder as she thought of what Uncle Daniel would do or say if she refused. None of these were necessarily the right reasons for failing to attend to her confession; however, they added a sense of doom to the thought of her next meeting with Father.

Giselle had news about the Chancellor's failure to visit Constance. A rift had sprung up between two neighboring landowners. He had spent hours in the Royal Throne room talking to each of them. They were reticent about listening to the acting King's counsel. A Regiment of Legionnaires was preparing to leave for the troubled area before there was bloodshed between the two men. Daniel decided to ride with the Legionnaires. A gala going forth ceremony was being prepared.

"What if he doesn't come back," Constance wailed.

"There are many men who will protect him. He is making sure this situation does not ferment into a war or bring in outsiders. His presence will make that clear," the Legionnaire said who was walking beside her as she descended to the Court Yard where the men were mustered. Daniel had sent for you to send them off with your approval. "That is why you are wearing the Royal Crest."

She had already figured that out when Giselle had laid out a beautiful Throne Room gown and slippers.

"What will I say?" she asked just before they reached the outer door.

"Chancellor Daniel will tell you."

Constance felt a different kind of shiver than the one she had felt at St. Stephen's. Since she had declared that her uncle would reign until she was age, she had never had to speak to the people again.

Her uncle met her at the door. He was splendidly attired. His chain mail shown brilliantly from a recent polishing. "Don't look so worried," he said to her as his eyes searched her taut face. "It is only an exercise in pomp and authority."

She knew instinctively that it was more than that. "What if you get hurt?"

"You will be queen sooner," he answered her honestly.

"No!" The word escaped her lips.

He put his hand up and covered her mouth, a gesture that brought back memories from when he had found her in the briars. "Yes," he hissed. Then he told her what to say to the Regimen to send them forth.

Bravely standing before the men and their horses, Constance repeated the words her uncle had told her to say. She ended by giving a Royal Blessing for each and all. A priest, hereto unknown to her, prayed and the group left in a cloud of dust with many people waving and cheering as they rode through town.

Constance was looking for a place to hide. She was scared and felt very alone. "Princess," the unknown priest was standing directly in front of her. She looked up at this stranger and saw peace in his eyes. "Friar, I am afraid," she said as she would say many times to this particular priest in the future. "Help me."

Back up in her room, she found a tense Giselle. "You are afraid too?" Constance asked.

"Little one," Giselle was helping her remove her ceremonial gown. "Any time the Legionnaires go out like that I am afraid."

Riding near the front of the regimen was a lithe lad, Ian by name. Daniel had designated him to be his personal servant in ordinary things. It would be the young man's first real test as to his bravery. "Thank you, Lord, for this grand excuse," Daniel was smiling as he rode along. He had missed the cavalier comradeship with the Legionnaires since assuming the temporary kingship. He felt as though he was years younger though he knew he would ache from the intense ride to the lands of the dissidents.

As for the young Ian, when summoned early that morning and told of the impending ride with the Legionnaires, the lad had only nodded and bowed to his orders. This little adventure would be the testing for that boy. If the young lad was to be given responsibility over the Princess, his obedience and valor needed to be proven.

Not a single courier brought back any information for the first fortnight. Constance made her confession to the priest at St. Stephen's. The Legionnaires kept especially close to Constance, one being beside, behind or in front of her every place she went except in her private rooms.

"Do you suppose something has happened?" she asked Giselle.

"The Holy Lord is in control."

"Why hasn't there been a courier telling us of their progress?"

Giselle turned away from the girl. She didn't want to think the worse yet even though she expected something from the Chancellor unless he was dead. Then she repented of that thought. A courier would hurry back and announce if there was bad news, she was certain.

The priest at St. Stephen's took sick suddenly. The priest, who had said the last prayer before the Legionnaires left, arrived early one morning. "I am Friar Joseph. I will teach you now."

"Will I be going to the Cathedral?" Constance asked.

"No, open the closed Chapel here in the castle. We will study there."

"I can do that?"

"Yes," he answered. "Your father closed the Chapel. It is appropriate that you open it."

Princess Constance made the declaration from the Throne Room.

Someone asked if Chancellor Daniel would approve.

"He is not here and I am the Princess." Constance responded firmly. *If he doesn't approve,* she thought, *he will close it when he returns.*

"How boldly she speaks!"

Constance smiled inwardly. *What they don't know is how afraid I am.*

The news came back from the distant quarreling landowners. The Legionnaires had gotten there in time to halt bloodshed although one of the landowners had hired mercenaries from a neighboring kingdom to patrol his lands. Daniel finally persuaded those men to return to their own kingdoms and required of the landowners to pay them a fair salary for their time and trouble. He also took from each of the quarreling households all of the young people for service under him with the promise that they would return home in ten years if the land owners maintained peace between each other.

There was no doubt that the Chancellor could have exacted a more serious penalty with the number of armed men with him. The women wailed and sobbed when he marched their offspring away.

"Will that be enough, Sire," one of his trusted men asked him. "If it is not, the next time I will burn their buildings as well as taking their flocks." Daniel's jaw was tight. Ian was riding beside him.

"Go on ahead and arrange for wagons in the next town to put the littler ones in," Daniel told him. "They do not have to suffer needlessly for the stubbornness of their fathers."

"What authority do I have to ask for wagons and horses?" Ian looked to Daniel.

Daniel lifted his lance with the crest from his saddle. "This," he said as he gave it to the lad. He was pleased that the lad recognized the need for a symbol of authority.

Ian took the lance, and urged his horse into a trot. "Go with him," Daniel said to two Legionnaires, "But let him do the negotiations."

At the next town, Ian went to the town square as the people gathered around him. "You are just a lad."

"That is the Kings lance!"

"Is he dead?"

"No," Ian answered when they allowed him to speak. "I was sent here to obtain wagons and horses."

"There has been bloodshed?"

"No, we have the children, some are very young. The Chancellor wants wagons and horses to take them back to the castle."

There was a commotion. "Why are those Legionnaires sitting over there in the trees?"

Ian shrugged his shoulders for he had not known of the two Daniel had sent behind him. "Ask them," he answered.

Several of the men approached the Legionnaires. "Why have you come?"

"Have you done as the lad asked," they answered.

The men looked at each other and shook their heads. "He is just a boy."

"He represents the King." The two Legionnaires shifted on the horses as though ready to become more aggressive.

"How many wagons?" One man asked.

"Ask the lad."

The men returned to those gathered around Ian. They were aware of the two Legionnaires following them on horseback.

"How many wagons?"

"Three," Ian stated, "plus horses and drivers."

"Drivers," someone muttered.

Ian nodded. "You can have the wagons and horses back as soon as we get to the castle."

There was some murmuring before three men volunteered to drive their wagons for the Chancellor.

Ian touched the lance tip to the ground in acknowledgement, bid them to be ready in the morning, and then turn his horse toward the Legionnaires. The three rode back toward where the slow-moving travelers were.

Before the sun rose the next morning, three wagons lumbered to the edge of where the Legionnaires were camped. Ian went to meet them as the Chancellor had instructed him. "Turn your wagons. I will get the children," he said. Upon returning to the Chancellor's camp, he found him awake and alert. "Which children?" Ian asked after bowing before his Lord.

"All those eleven years and under plus the one who is crippled. As soon as they are loaded, have the wagons go on ahead. You will walk with the wagons and the walking children."

"My mount, Sire?"

"The Legionnaires that follow closely will bring your horse."

"Sire, that is a punishing distance for all those children to walk."

"And you?" Daniel looked at the lad. In his mind were the words, *discipline and pain*.

"I am prepared for the walk," Ian answered and bowed.

"Use your judgment when it is time to place others into the wagon. They must not be made lame but they must understand the hand that is over them." After a short pause, he stated, "Kneel."

Ian knelt while the Chancellor placed his hand of authority on the lad.

The younger children of the older ones whimpered when they were not bidden to get into the wagon also. Ian stared at them remembering how frightened and ill equipped he had felt the first time he had watch a flock over night at home. From then on, he kept his eyes turned away from them fearing they would see his compassion for them and thereby try to manipulate him.

The wagons pulled out with the smallest of the children and the rest followed behind walking and just out of sight, a group of Legionnaires followed on horseback often pausing so that they did not draw close to Ian, the wagons and the walking children. The children would be a long time walking before they even stopped for a meal.

The Chancellor sent one group of Legionnaires by another way to reach the castle more quickly. The rest he kept with himself, sending spies back to report on the two landowners whose children he had taken. One lone courier was sent back to the castle in a hurry to report the news.

Constance received the courier formally in the Throne Room. The room was crowded with many wanting to hear the news. The courier spoke to her in quiet tones and the crowd shifted trying to draw closed to hear. Constance, at the urging of one of the Legionnaires who was protecting her, ordered the Throne Room cleared of everyone but herself, the courier and the two men who were constantly with her.

"The Chancellor is well. There has been no bloodshed. Three wagons of children plus the older children are coming here. It will take a fortnight for them to get here. The Chancellor wants the children to be housed by the church, and isolated as well, until he is here."

"He is not coming back?" blurted out Constance.

"Some of the regimen will be here in two days," the courier continued. "He is waiting behind so that there is not an attempt to rescue the children from captivity." The courier then stepped closely to Constance speaking softly, "He urges you to be courageous of heart and mind. He said for you to tell the people that all is well, which they will receive with gladness. When the first group of Legionnaires arrive, there will be more to tell them."

Friar Joseph paled but nodded when Constance reported all that the courier had told her. "The monastery will be made ready to receive the children. Have you spoken to the people?"

"A crier is in the city now spreading the news." She looked down at her shaking hands, "I am so afraid."

"Do you not believe what the Chancellor has told you?"

She looked up quickly and was held by the intense gaze of the friar. She was aware that she had blushed at his question and started to turn away.

His outreached hand stopped her. "Do not run. Trust."

She shook as emotions over ran her senses. She dared not say what was on her mind. *Whom do I turn to?* Friar Joseph had already drilled her to know that answer even if she didn't like it. Her faith was still that of a frail child.

At Giselle's knees, Constance wept as she lamented her lost childhood. The wise woman caressed her and urged her to wear her diamond-studded hairpin.

Meeting

*I*an enjoyed his foray with the Legionnaires so when the children were safely in the hands of the friars and monks, he had felt lost when it was evident that he was still just a lad in service to the Chancellor. He returned to the room that had been his, the turret, and spent hours gazing out at the spires. Ian felt a deep loss because of the sickness of the priest at St. Stephens.

Ralle encouraged him to mingle with the other younger men that served the Chancellor only. They seemed like boys compared to the Legionnaires he had been with. He was in the stables tending to his mount when the news came that the Chancellor was at the edge of the city. The town was alive with the crowds massing along the route to the castle. He took a position near the castle and waited.

When the Chancellor appeared, the crowds roared. Ian waved as the Chancellor rode by. Daniel caught a glimpse of the young man as he rode on into the castle. As he had done when he brought the errant princess home several years earlier, the Chancellor rode his horse into the throne room before dismounting. The hardstone floor echoed the sounds of the prancing of the spirited horse. He walked to the Throne and sat down. The roar of the crowd who had followed him in was deafening. "Bring me the lad who tended the children," he ordered his courier.

Ian quickly appeared before him and bowed low to the Chancellor.

"Welcome home," the lad said as Daniel embraced him and thanked him for bring the children safely to the city.

"Where is Constance?" the Chancellor asked when he realized she was not present.

Several of the couriers looked at each other hoping one of them knew the answer. Finally, one answered. She is in her room."

"No one told her I was home?" There was a slight twitter among those standing around that Daniel ignored. Various officials of his court were standing by waiting to report to him. He turned to them.

Some said that he was annoyed by her lack of presence but others thought it was prudent that he spent his time making sure that all was well with the kingdom. Neither of the excuses for the lack of the princess nor the apparent lack of concern by the Chancellor was correct.

Daniel spent the first days after his return to the castle resting and thinking. Constance was fourteen now and Ian was more than seventeen. It was time to move into the next phase of bringing up his niece. Ian's maturity had grown with the task of transporting the children. Daniel knew he had no fears of placing Ian with Constance to be the young woman's companion and protector. *Too bad he is not of royal blood,* he thought. It was too soon to be thinking of her marriage and he blushed, even as he had briefly considered what kind of man would make his headstrong niece a good husband. "Don't rush things," he told himself out loud. "She is still mostly child."

Constance was shaking from the anticipation of a private meeting with her uncle. In her mind, she remembered her escapade that he had never confronted. *Would he now?*

"Stand still or I will never get this gown buttoned up correctly!" Giselle admonished her. "Why we let the seamstress add all these buttons, I don't know."

"She thought it would look pretty," Constance answered her absent-mindedly.

"And cause me stress," Giselle struggled with one button loop. "We are going to only open the buttons that will let you safely get out of this dress when you take it off."

Constance giggled. "What if I open all of them?"

Giselle reached up and pinched Constance. That instantly brought Constance back to the scheduled private meeting with her uncle. "Ouch!"

"You will get more than that if you don't stop wiggling," Giselle answered harshly as she knelt on the floor to finish the long line of buttons.

Constance was silent. A long string of memories rushed through her mind. "What if he is still mad at me for hiding in the garden?" she whispered.

"Then I suppose he will have to undo all these buttons to get you into a dressing gown so he can whip you." The conversation went on much too casually for Constance.

She stomped her foot. "Stop that!" she exclaimed.

Giselle had moved in time not to be hit by the girl's foot. "You do that again, and I will whip you."

Constance cried.

"Oh, my poor child," Giselle reached out and stroked her back. "I was just talking, forgive me,"

Constance nodded through her tears. Giselle handed her a handkerchief with which to blot her eyes.

"It will never do for the Chancellor to see you coming in tears."

Again, the girl nodded. "I am so afraid."

Inwardly, Giselle rejoiced that her charge was expressing her fears and that they seemed to be sincere. She also could imagine being rebuked for causing the princess to cry before her visit with the Chancellor. Some of the girl's fear was contagious.

The Chancellor was pacing the floor in his private chambers. Constance was late. He pondered, *what does this mean?* He was of a mind to go to the girl's rooms and see what was taking her so long to answer his summons when there was a knock on the door and his courier announced, "The Princess Constance." She was beautiful in her long formal gown. The sparkle of the lone diamond hairpin caught his eye. He remembered his cousin presenting it to Constance. And unbidden, he also remembered that Constance had cause considerable grief for her caretakers that night. He wondered if she even remembered her disobedience.

"My Lord and Sire," Constance curtseyed gracefully before him.

"I understand that the kingdom was well in my absence?"

"Yes, Sire," she answered quietly. "Your throne remained intact."

"Who taught you how to say that?"

The question took Constance by surprise. She hesitated for a brief moment. "Friar Joseph. He is teaching me here in the castle."

Daniel knew that but waiting in silence to see if she had more to say.

"The priest at St. Stephen's is ill."

Nodding to her comment he continued to remain silent.

"The chapel here in the castle is being restored. The one my father closed years ago. I go there daily for my lessons."

"You decreed it to be restored?" her uncle was watching her closely.

"Forgive me if it is not your desire also." She inclined her head slightly.

He stepped closer to Constance and saw her movement of fear as he reached out to her. He embraced her. "I am pleased that it is being restored."

His embrace had shaken her. As he continued to hold her, she felt the warmth of his love. "Thank you, Sire."

"Uncle Daniel," he replied and stepped back.

Constance's face lost the fearful look she had when she first entered into his presence.

"But I see that you are remembering your escapade when my cousin was here."

The look of fear in her eyes returned again. Constance dropped her gaze as her shoulders slumped.

"Constance," Daniel called her name so that she would look up at him. "That was another time, another place. It is time to move on."

A puzzled look was now on her face.

"Soon, I will introduce the lad who is to be your constant companion, in schooling and other daily activities as you move about more freely. I trust him. Do not do anything to cause my trust in him to be shaken.

"You are to return to your private quarters where you have lived since your childhood. He will reside in a room nearby. Only when you are in your private quarters will he not be present with you. Giselle will still remain 'your lady'. I have replaced all those who were in your private rooms before. It is best that no one be there that remembers the disobedient child you were with the exception of Giselle."

In the silence after Daniel stopped speaking, Constance's mind was racing. She did not have to beg to get her private rooms back. Her uncle had given her a gift, like his cousin had. Unmerited! A strange emotion overcame her and she sobbed.   The Chancellor, watched as she sorted out her emotions. As her uncle, he was very proud of her. This was the first time he had looked at her as the future Queen without seeing the spoiled child. He realized he was feeling emotional also.

"Show me the chapel that is being renovated."

Constance placed her hand on his bent elbow as they left his private rooms. Two Legionnaires fell in behind them. They noticed how easily the girl and her uncle fit together as the ruler and future ruler of the kingdom. Later, they discussed it between them and with the other Legionnaires.

Daniel was surprised when they reached the chapel. It was actually complete with all the beauty that had been there before was already fully restored. Both he and the young Princess knelt before the altar in silent prayer. Daniel's thoughts went back to the destruction and closing of the chapel years before. Constance's mind sought answers to all that her uncle had just told her.

"I am so glad you had the Holy Chapel restored." Daniel shared with her as they returned to his private rooms.

"Friar Joseph told me to do it," she murmured.

A wise man, Daniel thought in his mind.

Giselle received the word of the move back to the Princess' original suite. She supervised the women who came to pack up Constance's dresses. She was too busy to wonder how the young girl was doing with her uncle. The courier had told her that she was the only remaining servant for Constance. All the rest were assigned elsewhere. Giselle noticed she did not know any of those who came to help them move. Who is going to be in charge, she wanted to ask? When the new women all turned to her before doing anything, Giselle realized she was the one in charge. It frightened her. *I have no experience,* she thought to herself forgetting the many months of being the only one in charge of Constance.

Ian was not surprised when the Chancellor sent for him early one morning. He dressed carefully each day in anticipation of the Chancellor's summons. He found himself a little nervous which he tried to chase from his mind. It was still lurking when he entered the presence of the King. He bowed and waited.

"I have a report about the children. They are doing well and they want you to visit them."

It was a surprise that this was the topic the Chancellor had taken with Ian. "Sire, if that in your wish, I shall."

"Your studies have been interrupted by the illness of the priest at St. Stephens. From now on, Friar Joseph will meet with you in the Royal Chapel to continue your studies."

Ian bowed to the decree.

"You also will meet the princess, the future queen, in the Royal Gardens soon to begin your service to me, her uncle and for her."

Ian scarcely dared to breathe.

"You have nothing to say?"

"Sire, I am overwhelmed. Forgive me if I seem a stumbling muted ox."

"An ox you are not," Daniel threw back at him. "Muted out of surprise or fear?"

Ian swallowed hard before he spoke again. "I have not dared think of this part of my service to you for fear that I was dreaming."

His king roared in laughter. "Of maybe you have heard too much of her childish behavior from the others?"

"Only the incident when I was still a page in the Royal Throne Room, Sire." Ian dropped his eyes as he also remembered all the other stories that had been cautiously discussed among the others in service to the Chancellor and the Legionnaires who had talked a little more freely.

"Why are you hiding your eyes from me, lad?"

Ian felt the fear that had been lurking jump onto his shoulder and scream in his ears. He attempted to maintain a neutral expression on his face as he raised his eyes back to the Chancellor. The instant that they connected with the gaze coming from Daniel, Ian knew that he had seen through his lie. "Forgive me, Sire, I lied to you." He dropped down to his knees.

Daniel moved away from the kneeling lad. He had fully expected him to deny knowing anything, but the boy's confession and complete submission was a surprise. "Evidently, I have chosen," and the Chancellor paused deliberately to watch via a mirror the boy who was still kneeling. Ian did not move but remained with his head bowed. "The correct person to be the companion for the Princess Constance." Ian's head came up as the

Chancellor turned back around. "I have not made a mistake in my choice. Remember this moment if you are tempted to fail me in anyway with her."

Daniel lightly touched Ian's head. "Go make your confession to Friar Joseph. You are dismissed."

The seasonal rains came. Daniel postponed the rendezvous in the Royal Gardens. Both Ian and Constance were tense and irritable. Constance's time was spent in renovating some of the older parts of her childhood chambers to fit her new and maturing personality.

Saddened by the move from the turret room to his new quarters, Ian was often found at the window of the turret praying. Friar Joseph took great pains in making sure the two young people never saw each other in the Royal Chapel.

At last the sun shone again, and all those tired of restricted activities outdoors went forth to enjoy the respite for one sunny day did not guarantee that the next would be without rain. The Chancellor cancelled all but activities in the Throne Room that were not essential to the kingdom.

Constance looked out her windows at the sparklingly bright sunlight. "What do you wish to wear?" Giselle asked her knowing that the girl had been trying on different gowns for her walk in the Royal Garden with her uncle.

The girl stood paralyzed before her many choices. "You pick the one," she answered after a while.

"What do you think your uncle would like?" Giselle was tormenting her.

"The yellow one, yellow like the sunshine and the flowers."

"And what if the lad does not like yellow?" Giselle asked.

"He will because I am wearing it," the girl answered with all confidence.

Giselle hid her smile as she got the designated gown ready for the young princess.

Ian was wearing the crest of the King on his sleeve. It was an honor for a servant to be allowed that privilege. He had been awake since before dawn when the rains had stopped. He yawned at breakfast and the manservant who now attended him laughed. "Yawning at this hour? What will the Chancellor think of you?"

Ian was not used to having someone around when he was just getting started in the morning. He looked at the man and saw him laugh at his own comment. He shrugged his shoulders.

"Oh, did the cat get in and take your tongue?" his companion egged him.

"No!" Ian answered a bit too forcefully. He ducked his head. "Sorry," he murmured.

Laurence grinned back. "Touchy too."

"No," answered Ian again in a more civilized tone.

The Chancellor's Courier knocked at the door. "His Majesty wishes to speak with you in his private rooms."

Ian used the napkin that he was just getting familiar with to wipe his mouth and followed the Courier back to the Chancellor's chambers.

Daniel was still eating his own breakfast. He offered Ian an orange slice.

Ian hesitated for an instant before happily devouring it.

"Are you ready, lad?"

"Sire? Yes, Sire." He decided he had better answer in the positive.

"Afraid?"

Ian looked at the Chancellor almost in surprise at the blunt question."

"Yes, Sire."

"You are her protector and guardian when the two of you are together. She can suggest, but your word is the last one. Be sure you remember that."

Ian nodded as he was in the middle of another orange slice the Chancellor handed him.

"Good, when my Courier comes for you, you will follow him to the Royal Gardens and wait near the Angel Statue. All the main paths start and stop there. She will enter by one of them."

Constance was mystified when her uncle called her to the Throne Room late in the morning. "I thought we would walk into the Gardens from here since this is the room you were watching that night from the garden."

A quick sideways glance did not reveal any other motive in her uncle except as he had just stated. Since Constance had never been in the gardens from this point before, she was confused as to where her favorite places of the garden were. After admiring the freshly blooming flowers and the brightness of the day, Daniel stopped at a junction in the paths.

"This one goes to the outer wall, that one takes a round- about way to the spot where you were hiding that night and this one goes to the Angel statue. Which one do you want to walk on first?"

Constance was torn. The one to the outer wall might be where she first saw the lad, but the one to her hiding place could be the one she should go to. "This one to the angel statue," she made her decision suddenly. "I so love that statue," she said.

Daniel nodded. This was easier than he had thought it might be. "We will go there but maybe we will stop before we get there.

"Stop teasing me, Uncle Daniel!" she declared.

He looked at her and laughed. "I was just trying to give you the full benefit of my assistance."

He let her take the lead on the path. She turned back once and told him to hurry up. He didn't but stopped to look at every flower that had burst forth that day.

He heard her 'oh' when she had gotten to the statue. He knew Ian was there. He turned back with a smile.

Ian was astounded by the beauty and maturity of the Princess. The stories had made her out to be just a child. The Princess was not a child.

"You are him, ah he," she corrected herself in grammar.

"Who else were you expecting?" he tossed back before he remembered she was the Princess. His face reddened as he then bowed to her.

"What is your name?"

"Ian, my princess," he answered.

"Mine is Constance, but then you already know that."

They stood looking at each other. "We are supposed to be companions," Ian answered.

"Humhuh," she answered in her best non-princess language. "So, call me, uh, Constance, no princess to it."

"I am just Ian," he replied.

"I like this statue the best of all of the statues in the gardens. Have you seen all of them?"

"No."

She led him down another of the paths; stopping to explain whatever statue they came upon.

It was nearly dark when the Chancellor sent his couriers into the

Royal Gardens to locate them. They were at the low wall over which many months before they had first seen each other.

Daniel smiled to himself. He also reminded himself to have Friar Joseph to start teaching them together the next day.

Companionship

*I*n the first few weeks together, they found great joy, both being in need of companionship. Friar Joseph found them to be challenging and very competitive with each other in their lessons, both of the Church and academic lessons. It was a stimulation which he enjoyed also as he tried to stump them with deeper and more complex ideas. When he succeeded in puzzling them, usually one or the other tried to formulate an answer. He watched the other pupil closely and found that he or she would often refute the attempted answer of the first with a complex and deeper understand than the other.

Ian was ahead of the Princess in Church understanding but she was closing the gap rapidly. The Friar noticed the differences as he spurred them on in their growth.

During the afternoons, the pair strolled in the Royal Gardens until Constance got bored with the same activity every day.

"Let us walk in the meadows," she challenged Ian one afternoon. He was agreeable until then were on the far side and she seemed to be headed to the woody areas.

"No, Constance," he had to say for the first time.

"Why not?" she challenged back.

"There may be danger lurking in the woods," he responded. He had stopped walking. She was a few feet ahead of him.

"I have been in the woods many times. There is no danger."

For the first time, Ian realized that she was challenging the authority that the Chancellor had given him.

"No," he answered more emphatically.

She took a step forward towards the woods. Ian found himself reaching out and taking her hand and giving her a little tug back towards the meadow.

"Stop that," she pulled her hand away.

"I will race you to the other side of the meadow." Ian responded again taking her hand. "I will even let you have a head start."

The idea of a challenge appealed to Constance. "Count to ten before you start," she set the rule.

"I will."

"Promise?" she asked.

He nodded as she began running toward the other side of the meadow. He watched her go and then started running after her. He caught her on the slight upslope of the next meadow. She had slowed down considerable when her skirts tangled in the deep grass where the two meadows met.

"That's not fair!" she struggled to free herself from his arms. He laughed and held her until in her struggle she pulled them both to the ground.

"The grasses got in the way," she said as she sat up after their fall.

"Not to mention your skirts," he laughed back.

"If I had on breeches, I could have beat you," Constance was determined to have the last word.

"Maybe," Ian offered her his hand and helped her up. She stood picking long grass stalks off of her gown.

"You were supposed to let me win because I am the princess."

Ian smiled but kept silent.

They walked side-by-side back to the castle, each deep in their own thoughts.

The race and tumble in the meadow was duly reported to the Chancellor. He had been surprised that it had taken Constance several weeks before she had issued a challenge to her constant daytime partner.

One morning during lessons, Ian was getting all the answers right. Constance had grown more and more silent as the discussion and questions continued. The Friar was aware of the increase of a pout on her face. She threw down her book saying, "I don't want to study now!"

"Then I suppose you need to spend time before the Holy Altar."

"No." The instant the word was out of her mouth, she saw Ian glance at the priest. "And you can't make me," she challenged.

"As your spiritual guide, I can recommend it strongly."

Ian watched the hereto-gentle priest become amazingly fierce. The authority of God radiated from his eyes.

"Go recite your prayers in front of the Altar. When you are ready, I will hear your confession."

Turning to Ian, "Come lad, we will pray for our princess before the Virgin Mary."

Constance found herself alone. After a while she went to where the Friar had instructed and prayed. She did not abandon her anger until she became aware that others were saying the midday prayers in the chapel. When she rose to leave with those who had come to pray, the Friar stood blocking her way. "Your confession," he said softly.

Constance made a negative sound before following him obediently to the Confessional. Ian waited patiently in a far corner of the chapel pondering the rebelliousness of his companion. Upon receiving a report from the Friar, Daniel was saddened and hid the events in his heart.

Company had come to visit the kingdom. The Chancellor requested Constance's presence at many of the functions that left Ian standing on the sideline watching. A few times Ian was frustrated when he saw the Pages active in the various ceremonies. He realized that he missed that part of the Page duties.

This was the third day of escorting the Princess Constance to the Royal Throne Room and then spending long hours just watching. The Legionnaires who always accompanied them were outside. In a way, he resented them and the freedom they had between times they were escorting the Princess.

Growing tired, Ian slipped out through one of the arches of the Royal Throne Room. As he stepped into the narrow hallway, he suddenly found himself pinned to the rough wall by a gloved hand. Barely able to turn his face from the wall, he could see that the one holding him was a Legionnaire.

"What are you doing out here?" a gruff voice asked.

Ian was mute not only from fright of the hand that was forcibly holding him to the wall but also not knowing how to answer the question.

The hand pushed him harder against the wall. "Answer me!"

"Turn him around," another voice interjected.

Roughly he was turned until he was standing looking into the face of the Legionnaire. He could see another one standing just behind the first one.

In the dim lighting in the narrow hall, Ian was sure they could not see the crest that he wore on his sleeve. "I am in service to the Chancellor," he managed to say.

"Don't lie to us, boy!"

"I wear the Royal Crest," he barely got out before the huge hand cuffed him across the head.

"You stole it!"

The blow had left Ian with tears in his eyes and a ringing in his ears. "No, Sire. The Chancellor put it on me."

"What is going on here?" a third voice asked.

"This boy was sneaking down this hallway."

The third Legionnaire peered into Ian's face. "I know the lad, let him go."

Ian nearly slipped down the wall when the forceful hold was released. "Why are you out here, lad?" the third voice asked.

"The Princess is occupied. I thought," Ian didn't get any further.

The sneering laugh of the one who had been holding him to the wall broke in. "You thought?"

"Leave him alone," the third voice commanded. "He is in service to the Chancellor. See the crest on his shoulder?"

There was a slight scuffing sound as the first two men backed away.

Quickly Ian was escorted back into the shadows of the Throne Room where he could watch the events taking place. As the rescuing Legionnaire hovered nearby, Ian had no desire to slip out again.

Ian and she were standing in the entrance room of Constance's chambers. It was the only room where he was allowed. "Then go ask him," she spouted back.

Ian hesitated. "You are afraid to ask him!" She exclaimed, her face right in his face.

"No, but with the attitude you have, I am not taking you out riding." Ian would have left at this point if the Chancellor had not suddenly appeared at his niece's rooms.

"What is going on?" Daniel asked in innocence.

"I want to go riding but he won't take me." She pointed an accusing finger at Ian.

"The reason," Daniel turned his gaze toward Ian.

"Permission, Sire." He did not mention attitude as a factor hoping that the Chancellor would see that.

"Permission granted, use a lady's saddle for Constance. The dapple-gray horse takes well to it."

Ian could barely control his smile as he realized what the Chancellor had instructed. He inclined his head.

For a brief moment, Constance had missed the sidesaddle instructions. "I don't want to ride that way!" she burst forth.

Her uncle turned his eyes toward her. "You will or you won't ride." Tension stretched its tight cord in the room. Turning his eyes back to Ian, he said, "You are dismissed."

Ian bowed and left grateful not to remain in the room. Once outside, he hurried the twenty or so feet to his own room. Laurence was there. "I did not expect you back so soon." His man was in the middle of housekeeping chores.

Ian waved his hand and sat down on a chair out of the way. He did not want to think about the possible conflict between the Princess and Chancellor. It was well known that when you were dismissed and the tension was great between the two, that the Chancellor was extremely firm with his niece. He was glad that he had not the issue of saddle type to contend with the Princess. He sighed.

"Tired?" asked Laurence.

"No, relieved," Ian murmured under his breath.

A courier arrived later stating that Constance would not need his companionship for the afternoon.

Giselle had backed out of the room when the Chancellor arrived but heard the exchange between Ian, Daniel and Constance. She hid herself in a distant room when she heard the Chancellor dismiss Ian.

Daniel looked at his niece. "You have been very difficult of the last few days."

Constance was looking for an excuse. "Who is gossiping about me, my servants, that lad?

Daniel raised his hand to stop her. "There have been several reports."

"You are spying on me!" she accused.

"Prudently keeping track of what you do, yes."

Much to his surprise, she fell silent. Neither spoke for a long period, although he was watching her face carefully trying to determine how she was thinking. She was tensely waiting for the first blow. When it didn't come, she began to hope that he was not going to do anything.

"Go change to your dressing gown," he broke the silence.

She gasped but then obeyed. She was terrified for she remembered well the last time he had her change into a dressing gown.

He went into her private rooms after she had changed. There was nothing that she could read in his face. "Sit down," he said quietly, "and listen."

She whimpered when he reached over and closed the ornately carved door between her room and all the others.

"You are confined to this room for the rest of the day. No meal will be brought in, Giselle will only come to the door, but she will not enter. In the morning, we, you and I will talk."

Daniel, her uncle, left the room and she heard him apply the outside latch that never was used and pull the key from the door. He had locked her in! Anger flooded her. She yelled and pounded at the locked door. After a period of time, she realized that no one could hear her nor would they disobey the Chancellor's orders. In her exhaustion, she cried herself to sleep. It was dark in the room when she woke. All the luminaries had burned out. She was frightened not of the man who was disciplining her, but of all the things that seemed to attack in the dark. She wrapped herself in her quilts and huddled on the bed. In desperation, she began to repeat the prayers that the Friar had been teaching her. Sleep would not come. She would not know when dawn came for the darkness was that complete in her room.

She wakened to the sound of the key being inserted into the latch. At first, she thought she was just hearing things like all those sounds and voices that seemed to fill the darkness after her candles had burned out. A sliver of light shone as the door was opened and Giselle entered carrying a lantern.

"Is it morning," Constance asked as she squinted at the light.

"Yes, and you need to dress. The Friar is coming with the Chancellor."

"Oh," was all she could manage.

Twenty minutes later, with the room fully ablaze with luminaries, Constance was dressed. Giselle brushed her hair. The woman had said very little that was not necessary for her to get ready. *If the Friar is coming,* she reasoned to herself, *then Uncle Daniel is not going to beat me. Unless,* her mind went on, *the Friar wants to beat me too.* Although she knew that was not true, her thinking was fuzzy.

Breakfast was served in a windowed room. She could hardly concentrate on eating for watching the sunshine and the tops of the trees she could see across the meadow.

"Hurry Constance, they will be here soon," Giselle urged her.

"You have two visitors," the doorkeeper announced as Constance was hurrying through her breakfast.

"They can wait until I am done," the princess commented.

Two Friars were waiting when she entered the room. "Princess Constance," announced the doorkeeper.

She stopped abruptly. "Where is my uncle?" The words came out without thought.

"He will be here later," Friar Joseph responded. "This is Friar Justin." Constance turned to the Friar whom she had never seen before and was arrested by the love that poured forth from his countenance.

"Friar," she murmured acknowledgement.

"Princess," he replied.

There was awareness in Constance that this Friar knew everything about her and that he loved her in spite of herself. It left her speechless. She barely heard what Friar Joseph was saying. The words drifted through her consciousness "your personal confessor." She looked at Friar Joseph puzzled by what she thought she had heard.

"Friar?" was her response.

Friar Justin spoke. His voice was soft and melodic. "Princess, do you have a place where we can talk in private?" He was acutely aware of the many listening ears in her private chambers.

She nodded, "The library. Only men are not allowed to go in there."

"Even your priest?"

Constance felt confused. She had not slept well. Now a priest who wanted to talk in private in her chamber confronted her. She glanced over her shoulder and saw Giselle who inclined her head slightly. Giselle would stop her if she were to make a bad decision about her private rooms. "I will meet with you in that room," she declared. "Giselle, please clear the way."

Inside, Giselle's heart was leaping with joy. Her charge had made a very adult choice. Giselle hurried into the depths of the Princess's private chambers and herded all the young attending ladies to the back. She opened the library door as she passed back through to indicate the way was clear.

Friar Joseph was conversing with Friar Justin when Giselle reappeared with a nod to Constance. "Friar? We can go back now." the princess said. "And you also, Friar Joseph?"

"No, my lady, I will return to the Holy Chapel." He bowed slightly and left.

Father Justin accepted the chair that Constance indicated. He watched the young girl quietly shut the door behind them. After making the sign of the cross, he paused, still looking at her with those remarkable eyes of love. "Tell me, Princess, what happened last night."

A brief moment of fright passed over her before she was able to again look into those loving eyes and begin to talk.

"I behaved rather badly before my uncle," was where she started.

An hour or so later, Constance agreed with the Friar that she felt out of control at times, and those were the times when she was punished, sometimes quite severely by her uncle. "I knew your father and mother," the Friar inserted at this point. "Your mother had a difficult time with your father. She believed in Jesus Christ. I am not sure your father did. He had a hate-love relationship with her. Sometimes," here the Friar paused.

"Sometimes there was no reason for his anger and behavior."

"I am like my father? Constance asked.

"No," he said after thinking awhile. You are much different, except when you are out of control."

"Then that is why my uncle punishes me so." Constance was searching for a simple answer.

"I think not," he answered. "He is just fearful that you will be headstrong all your life, running into walls, and making unjust decisions or at least unwise ones."

"How do you know so much about him?" Constance was confused and yet satisfied with the Friar's assessment of her uncle.

"We talked all night."

"After he locked me in my room?"

Justin nodded.

"Oh." For the first time in her life she realized the pain her uncle was suffering as he disciplined her. "Discipline and pain," she said softly.

"He said that numerous times last night," the Friar murmured.

Without warning, Constance found herself sobbing in sorrow and shame. It happened when she had looked into the Friar's eyes again. She cried for a long period of time unaware of the Friar kneeling on the hardstone floor fervently praying for her deliverance from her anger and resulting disobedience.

When she quieted, Friar Justin spoke. "Would you like to make your confession now?"

For a brief moment, Constance wasn't sure that she had anything to confess, and then she nodded and knelt before the humble Friar.

As the late spring days turn hot and muggy, Constance and Ian rode in the late afternoon or early evening. This time was always a high light for Constance. She accepted riding sidesaddle on the gray dapple horse. The horse was very sensitive to every mood and feeling of his rider, even coming to a halt when she slipped on the saddle one day. Ian took her into the less dense woods on well-traveled paths where low hanging branches were not a danger.

"I thought you said that the woods were dangerous," she challenged Ian one afternoon.

He had been waiting for the comment. "There are Legionnaires nearby."

"Where?" She twisted her head and upper body around looking for them. Her horse stopped as she moved.

"Just out of sight. They check the woods before I ever bring you here. Now, look what you have done," Ian grinned. "Your horse has stopped because you are squirming around too much."

"Am not!" she said and urged her horse to a move on.

Ian laughed when the horse just stood as still as a statue. "I think he knows your attitude is wrong too."

A flash of anger welled up in her before she could stop it.

"Would you prefer to walk back, on your own two feet?" Ian had taken the reins from her hand.

Constance reached for the reins. Ian laid his riding crop across the back of her outstretched hand.

"No," he said.

She looked up at him and the crop that was now lying across her hand. He had not hit her with it but his placing it there was clear. As she sat on the big gray horse, inside her mind was raging.

She pulled her hand back and continued to sit, quietly.

After a time, Ian spoke. "Shall we ride back to the castle?"

Constance nodded. She felt ashamed of her challenge of Ian.

"Next time we ride, wear your breeches," he said to her as they left the stable.

"Aren't you afraid that I might ride recklessly?"

He only shook his head as they returned to the inside of the castle.

Daniel looked at the lad. "She what?"

"She became angry with me."

"You did nothing to provoke that anger?"

"No, Sire," Ian was looking straight at the Chancellor. "Only that I told her no."

The tension between the Chancellor and his special servant was high. "I assume you had good reason for telling her that."

Ian looked down briefly. "She was not obeying."

For Daniel, that explained it all. As her uncle, he knew of Constance's angry outbursts. "You do want not to take her riding?"

Ian shook his head. "No, Sire, I told her to wear her riding breeches next time. I am going to let her ride as a lad. There is a meadow over beyond the small woods that will be safe to let her try to keep her seat on that horse when she urges it to run."

"She did very well at that a few years ago." Daniel remembered her nearly killing his horse.

"The Legionnaires will be stationed in the woods nearby if she is that foolish." Ian paused. "Sire, she responded to my correction, I think she is ready for an adventure."

"Have you forgotten she is the future queen," Daniel looked Ian in the eye.

"No, Sire, she is a good rider and the gray is a good horse. He will not let her abuse him or hurt herself."

"You talk as though the horse has a mind like a human."

"Some horses are smarter than humans, Sire. That horse fully understands his rider. That is why she got angry with me."

Daniel was beginning to wonder about the lad talking to him. "Explain!"

"He knew she was angry and he refused to move."

After a slight pause, Daniel nodded. The best mounts he had had knew him as well as he knew himself. "Permission granted."

The summer passed quickly. Every so often Ian allowed the princess to ride like a lad. She was a skilled rider and a quick learner. The gray horse would not let her take chances.

"What have you told this horse about me," she complained to Ian one day after an exhilarating ride.

"That you are the Princess and that he must take care of you," Ian laughed.

She put a playful pout on her face.

"Be careful or you will walk back," he said as he urged his horse to a trot. Her horse continued at a walk.

"Now look what you have done," she called out to him as he pulled away. He circled back beside her, still grinning.

Ian turned eighteen and was eligible to begin training as a Legionnaire. It bothered him for he knew that someday, he would not be a part of the future Queen's intimate circle. He admired the Legionnaires and many of them were his friends. He knew he would not be content herding sheep in the mountains where he was born.

Daniel heard the young man out when he expressed his concerns and feelings about the princess and where his life was going. It grieved Daniel that Ian was not of royal blood for he had certainly fallen in love with Constance and understood her moods well.

Constance was fifteen. More was expected of her in the Royal Court. Some days, she spent long boring hours just being present for this visitor or that. When she complained, first to Ian and then to her uncle, she got no sympathy from either. "You will be the queen. Much is expected of you." Uncle Daniel had said that to her so many times that the words often intruded in her dreams during the night.

Realizing that not only Ian needed more challenge in his life, but also, if Constance was not to make up her own games of challenging him, he would have to find something more challenging than sitting around in the Royal Court. The Chancellor asked her one day. "Would you like to help with the little ones that are staying at the monastery?" He had explained previously why he had taken them from their homes until their father's agreed to agree. She had met several of the older ones who were learning skills from the shops near the monastery one day when she and Ian had taken a message to one of the shop owners. Characteristic of her age, she just shrugged her shoulders and didn't think about his question. Later, he sent for her and told her that she was going to be helping with those children at the monastery. Her first reaction was that he was jesting until the next morning when Giselle woke her before dawn and dressed her in a basic peasant's dress. Giselle repeated the detailed instructions that she had to abide with. "No one is to know you are the Princess. Answer all questions truthfully. Do not complain. Do whatever you are told to do. And, yes, you will come back to the castle nightly after dark escorted by a Legionnaire. Do you understand?"

Constance again shrugged her shoulders. She did not know that her time at the monastery would be a bigger challenge than sitting in the Royal Court all day long both to her and to the sister in charge.

"Oh yes, answer the sisters whenever they speak to you. Call them Sister unless they have told you their names. It is like the use of Friar or Sire here in the castle." Giselle gave her a little pat on the arm and sent her off with the waiting Legionnaire so that she would arrive while it was still dark.

As they went through the still dark streets, she wondered if Uncle Daniel was angry with her. Although he had tried to explain to her about learning about her future subjects, she did not connect this totally strange event that seemed to have overtaken her.

She had never been around children. Until Ian came into her life, her companions had been adults in submission to the King. Now she was expected to be in submission to the Sister in charge and to know how to do whatever was asked of her without revealing her identity. Sister Bridgett, who welcomed her as an extra pair of hands, had not been told that the new girl was the princess. Sister threw up her own hands up at the ignorance of this new helper. She had set Constance to scrubbing down the floors in the nurseries where the children slept while they were at breakfast that morning. Those rooms were always in need of cleaning with the number of children housed there. It was quickly evident that the new girl did not know the simplest rudiments of scrubbing a floor.

Sister stood with her hands on her hips, looking at the girl who was still standing basically where she had left her when she had taken the young children to the refectory. "Why have you not cleaned the floor?"

Constance looked at her in fear. "I don't know how, Sister."

"You are how old?" Sister was working herself up ready to scold the shiftless girl when one of the Friars happened by. After a quick glance at Constance, he could see her terror.

"Sister, this girl comes from an aristocratic family. She probably never has done any work like this."

"Then I will have to teach her how," Sister declared. "What is your name, child?"

Constance gulped. If she told her correct name, would the Sister guess she was that 'Constance'? The words of Giselle echoed in her memory, *always tell the truth*. "Constance." she answered with a slight curtsey."

The Sister saw the dip. "Who is you father?"

Again, it was a question that would give away her identity. "He is dead, Sister."

"I am sorry," the nun replied, "May God bless you."

The young woman definitely confounded Sister. "Yes. Sister?"

Sister Bridgett looked at the young girl. It was apparent that she did not come from a home where children never asked anything of an elder or a religious, but she was courteous.

"Show me what to do."

The nun, although a woman who was not prone to laughter, nearly laughed. "Have you any brothers or sisters?"

At this point, Constance's mind was wondering what the Chancellor was thinking, sending her to the monastery. It certainly was a different kind of disciple and pain. "No, Sister." Her answer was short.

The Friar was still standing nearby. "May I suggest Sister Aristina to train her."

Sister Bridgett's eyes snapped with anger as the friar had butted into the conversation again. She turned toward him and very civilly said, "That is impossible."

"Because she is a dreamer?" The friar pressed his point. "Let her take this girl and work with her in the classes she is teaching the children."

"Art and music?" Have you been schooled in these things?" she addressed Constance.

"Yes, Sister." Wanting to get on with the need to get the rooms mopped, and the dilemma that this young girl was causing her by her ineptness, the Sister nodded. "Very well. Do you know where Sister Aristina is?"

"Praying for a helper," the friar said. "I can take this young girl to her."

"Thank you, Friar," Sister Bridgett turned abruptly away from Constance and went into the room that needed mopping.

Constance hurried after the friar whose stride caused her to almost run to keep up. When they entered St. Stephen's he slowed down and genuflected. "Wait here, while I go get Sister Aristina."

Constance knelt and thanked God for the resolution of the problem that Sister Bridgett had with her and that no one seemed to guess she was the princess Constance.

She was not prepared for the tall nun who approached her a few minutes later. Sister's nose was long and aquiline, her eyebrows heavy, and her mouth a line of sternness. "Hello, Constance," the voice was smooth like honey and the eyes that looked at her were warm with love. For a moment, Constance just stood and took in the extreme opposites presented before her in the Sister, before she remembered her manners.

"Good morning, Sister," Constance did the slight curtsey dip that she had used with Sister Bridgett.

"Sister Aristida," the nun corrected.

"Beg our pardon, Sister Aristina." Constance acknowledged the correction.

"Do you draw, paint, sculpt, sing or play an instrument?"

Constance nodded. "All but sculpt, but I do like sculptures." She stopped suddenly before she said more.

"Good," the tall nun said. "God said he would provide. Many of the children have the gentler talents. That is something Sister Bridgett gets confused about." The sister started down the aisle of the church. "Come, the children will be restless if we are late."

A very tired Constance walked home after dark with two Legionnaires. "Come on sleepy, you are walking slower and slower."

Giselle was waiting with a hot bath, but Constance was asleep before she could get her into it. The next morning came much too early. Giselle asked her a few questions about what she had done and whom she had met. Constance concentrated on eating for she had learned the meals were very sparse at the monastery.

And, so the Princess began to learn about children, learning to meet their needs, disciplining them, comforting them and doing menial tasks that anyone tending children did. For the first time in her life, she saw children misbehaving in much as the same manner that once she had. One child was determined to run away. Constance had a compassionate heart for him. He was different, and determined. Several of the older children had tried early in their tenure at the monastery but after several sessions receiving severe punishments, they had settled down.

This boy was younger, very much a child and for the third time in one week he had taken off again, trying to lose himself in the city in hopes of returning to his home. Several thought they had seen him climb over the wall of the monastery on the side where St. Stephen's was. They assumed he was trying to hide in one of the many homes in the squalid area where pigs were raised. "If he isn't found before dark, he may make good his escape back to his father's place."

A dozen or so Legionnaires were called to help search for him. Constance was among those who were looking in the closer environs, hoping that he was just hiding in a dark spot of the monastery. She stepped into darkened church sanctuary, mostly to be away from the intense search. She could always say that she was praying for them to find the lad if anyone asked. She knelt before the altar. If they did find him, she knew how severely they would deal with him.

She heard a faint noise near the confessional. *I did not realize Friar was having confessions,* she thought to herself. She arose and walked over to the confessional. The small sign that changed whenever someone was in the confessional was not flipped up. *Maybe I am wrong,* she thought. Then she heard the noise again, only it seemed to come from the part where the friar was supposed to be,

"Friar?" she called out tentatively.

The faint noise happened again only muffled.

It was growing late in the afternoon and the lighting from the windows was rapidly waning. Soon, only the sanctuary lamp would be the brightest light in the church. She shivered from the feeling that someone else was in the church with her. She almost wished someone would come over from the monastery looking for her.

The rustling noise in the confessional occurred again. Then she thought she heard a whimper. *Rorde, the runaway?* she questioned in her mind. She went back to the confessional and pulled open the curtain. Curled in a corner was the boy his eyes big with fear and yet defiant at the same time. He attempted to run past her. She snagged hold of his thin shirt and then an arm to stop him. Constance found herself in a wrestling match with the child as he tried alternately kicking and biting her. She held on in spite of his efforts with the same fierceness that she had fought with her own capturers when she was younger.

"Let me go," he yelled at her. She felt her simple dress rip as he tried over and over to get her to release him.

"God, help me," she heard her voice cry out in the midst of the struggle.

One of the doors opened at the back. Constance hoped whoever had opened it would come on in. Seconds later, heavy footsteps ran up the aisle. A Legionnaire lifted the fighting boy out of Constance's grip and held him at arms-length away as the child kept on with his desperate fight. He swatted the boy with a heavy hand and the boy ceased his fight.

Another Legionnaire had arrived. "Who is that?" as he pointed to Constance who had collapsed after the boy was taken from her.

By now, the commotion in the church had attracted the other searchers. "The Princess!" a Legionnaire said.

Sister Bridgett had heard the remark as she came hurrying in as the word spread that the boy had been found. *The future Queen?* The words shot through her mind. She looked at Legionnaire in disbelief. It had never occurred to her that the Chancellor would send the Royal Princess to do menial work at the monastery. Sister Bridgett dropped down by Constance noting the tears in her dress and the bite marks on her arms. "You are the Princess?"

"Yes, Sister."

The nun would have involuntarily taken a step backward if she had been still standing. She felt faint. As she regained her composure, she asked, "Why are you here?" Constance wondered that herself. "Perhaps the Chancellor wants me to experience life as a servant," she replied with her eyes downcast.

Sister made the sign of the cross saying, "Lord have mercy," under her breath. *No wonder this girl did not know how to scrub floors!*

The Legionnaires had taken the boy outside. Another stepped forward. "I will take her back to the castle," he said indicating Constance.

She was sobbing into her injured hands. A Friar nodded agreement to the Legionnaire standing by Constance. "Carry her," he said softly as he made the sign of the cross over the stricken girl.

Within minutes a contingent of worried men carried the crying princess back to the castle. A very pale Giselle met them at the door of the private chambers. The one carrying her stepped inside.

Constance collapsed on an ornate lounging chair still in uncontrollable sobs.

"Guard the door," Giselle ordered without thinking that she had no right to do so. The man nodded and stepped outside where several of his comrades had already placed themselves on guard at the door.

A Friar approached and they stepped aside to allow him entrance. Giselle, bent over Constance, examining her wounds spoke without looking up. "I said let no one in!" she snapped as she heard the door open and close behind her. "Oh!" she found herself blushing when she saw who had entered. "Forgive my outburst, Friar."

He nodded and knelt by the princess. "May God bless you, Constance." He was tracing the sign of the cross on her forehead.

She opened her eyes and looked at him. Her tears ceased and within a few minutes she was sitting up.

Giselle wanted so badly to get to the wounds on Constance's arms but could not do so without undressing her. The Friar was speaking softly to the girl. Someone else came in the door. "I need to get her to her bedchamber," muttered the flustered servant. Giselle decided she needed to get her deeper into her private rooms since no one was honoring the girl's privacy.

"I will carry her," the Chancellor's voice answered.

Giselle stumbled in her curtsey to the Chancellor. "Sire, a thousand pardons, I beg of you for my presumptuous words." Daniel had his niece in his arms with the assistance of the Friar. *She is growing up,* he thought as he toted her to her bed.

After he had placed her down, Daniel straightened cautiously.

"Are you?" He cut the Friar off with a brusque nod.

The Friar returned to the greeting room, the first room, and waited. A few minutes later, the Chancellor joined him. "I had no idea," he started to say before covering his face with his hands.

Constance slept fitfully. She woke once to ask about the plain dress she had been wearing. "It is a rag now," Giselle stated.

"No! Wash it! Mend it! I will return wearing it!" To keep her calm, Giselle picked up the dress that she had thrown into a corner. It was torn and some of the wounds on the girl's arms had left bloodstains. She shook her head in dismay.

Three days after the attack, Constance was up before daybreak. "Where is my dress?" Giselle offered her a similar one without all the repairs, and faint stains. "I want the one I was wearing!" The stubbornness of the princess was very evident. Giselle relented in obedience and dressed her in the marred peasant's dress.

The Legionnaires who walked with her to the monastery were silent when she asked about the young boy who had hurt her so. After spending a few minutes in St. Stephen's, Constance went looking for Sister Aristida.

"I am seeing a ghost," the nun exclaimed when Constance found her at last.

"I hurt too much to be a ghost," Constance answered back. "Where is the boy, Rorde?"

A guarded look came over Sister Aristida's face. She had been forbidden to talk about him.

"Well?" Constance persisted.

"Ask Sister Bridgett," the nun finally said.

"Is she the one who is not allowing you to tell me where he is?"

"Oh, no, Constance. The Friar gave that order," Sister Aristida answered before she gasped realizing she had said too much.

"He is dead?"

The sister turned her head away.

Constance felt frustrated. "Which Friar?" she demanded. Aristida seemed deaf to her question.

"The children are waiting," a voice interrupted their conversation.

Aristida nodded. "Come Constance, we must keep their minds and hands busy."

Constance turned to see who had entered the room with them. "Sister?" Constance was ready to ask another about the boy and yet she felt inclined to remain silent. She puzzled over her change of mind as she hurried behind the tall sister to the room where the children were waiting for directions. Instant silence greeted Sister Aristida when she entered, then, they saw Constance. Constance smiled at them and saw the worry on their faces turn to joy. She knew she was doing the right thing to come back to them.

One little girl came up to her as she was helping another arrange some flowers for the sanctuary and tugged on her sleeve. The painful wound inside the sleeve hurt but just for a moment when the girl smiled and said, "We missed you." Tears sprang to Constance's eyes as she ducked her head so that the girl wouldn't see them.

She helped several carry the flowers over to St. Stephen's. A Friar whom she did not know was busy until he saw her and the children come in. He came over and told the children to place the flowers at the feet of the Virgin Mary statue. Constance stood back and watched.

She picked one flower that had fallen out of an arrangement and knelt before the Virgin. She laid the flower across the outstretched hands of the statue.

The Friar started to say something, but elected to remain silent as he listened to her petition to the Virgin. "Mary, I don't know where the little boy, Roade, is but you do. Please tell him that I forgive him. I know how scared he was." Tears watered the lone flower.

Runaway

B y the middle of her sixteenth year, the Chancellor was looking at a maturing young woman who was falling in love with her companion. It was time to do something different. Her moody, difficult days were mostly behind her. He planned a special evening of riding, eating in the Royal Garden and a long talk with the two of them.

Two days before the planned party, Ian and Constance went riding earlier than usual. When they had not returned by dusk, the Chancellor sent for his trusted Legionnaires. He quizzed those who often rode just out of sight but in the same area that the two usually took. "They slipped away from us," the shamefaced men reported.

"Has this happened before?"

"Yes, but they have always returned." The Legionnaires were on their knees in submission to their King.

"Why did you not tell me?" The anger in the Chancellor's eyes frightened them. "Find them and bring them home!"

A day passed and there still was no Ian or Constance. Neither the Chancellor nor Giselle had slept much. One worrying and the other growing angrier with his niece as time passed. The Royal Legionnaires fanned out over the countryside, stopping at every farm and inquiring. The bad news was that there were highwaymen reported in the area. Should they tell the Chancellor about the robbers, or just keep that information to themselves?

In Daniel's mind, Constance was pulling her biggest hide and seek game ever and he had thought she was maturing. Her dress was found tangled in some briary bushes. There was blood on it. The Legionnaires shuddered at the thought of the princess possibly being dead. Those who were most responsible for shadowing the couple were terrified.

"Isn't this where Daniel used to have a cave he used?" one asked the others.

"Let's find that cave. The princess has been in it with Daniel. That is where he took her when he found her that day."

Energized they began to search the area until one called out. "Here it is!"

"We will need torches." They gathered at the entrance to the cave.

"Send someone to the other entrance," another one recalled that Daniel had two ways into the cave.

"Shall we notify the Chancellor?" The others looked at the speaker and shook their heads. "It may all be for nothing. He is in such a rage now." The others nodded in agreement.

Ian and Constance were frightened because they could hear men shouting back and forth. They had no idea who the men were.   T h e y had crept as far back into the cave as they dared without a light. Now they clung to each other, he shielding her from view of those who might find them inside. When the Legionnaires found them, Ian tried his best to protect Constance, until they subdued him and bound him hand and foot. They carried the fighting Constance half naked out of the cave. A Legionnaire threw a cloak over the frightened girl and hauled her up on the horse with him. They threw the bound Ian over one of the other horses and started at a trot toward the castle. It was a rough trip for each of them.

They were carried unceremoniously into the Chancellor's private chambers and dropped on the floor. Daniel's face was nearly purple from his rage at their behavior. He ordered Ian unbound. The lad immediately dropped to his knees in total submission before the Chancellor. Daniel stared at Constance's torn and soiled undergarments until she picked up the wrap that had been around her and covered herself.

Daniel sent all but two Legionnaires from the room. He picked up a whip that lay coiled on a side table. Constance gasped as he flexed his arm. "I am going to whip you until ..."

"No," Constance cried out. "He did nothing to me, Uncle Daniel. He was protecting me!" In his submission, Ian did not flinch a muscle as the raging Chancellor raised his arm.

Constance was furious. "Uncle, why do you assume we have done something wrong?"

Daniel's glare turned toward his niece. "You will feel the whip also." Her defiant attitude angered him.

"Then strike me first," she challenged. Dropping the garment, she had been covering herself with, she moved to place herself between Daniel and Ian.

"Sire?" The Legionnaire standing closest and a lifelong friend of Daniel spoke up softly. "Listen to what she has to say. The future of the Queen and the Kingdom are at risk."

Daniel, near exhaustion from his worry and anger, looked at his old friend.

Constance snatched the momentary lull to speak and to tell what had happened to her. "Uncle, Ian and I were attacked by some highwaymen. They took our horses. We ran in to the briary woods to get away from them. My gown snagged and I was caught in the briars until Ian torn my gown off of me so that we could get away. It was dark and they lost sight of us. When dawn came, I recognized the woods. It was where you found me caught in the briars.

"I knew there was a cave somewhere nearby. We could hear the highwaymen starting to look for us again. We found the cave and hid. That is where the Legionnaires found us only, we did not know they were Legionnaires. The cave was dark. Ian tried to protect me. The beat him and bound him and carried us back here. He was only trying to protect me."

Daniel was staring at his niece. Her determination to sacrifice herself for Ian was admirable but it was the foolish stuff young love was made of. Then he remembered a love that had sacrificed herself for him so that he could get away from the deadly wrath of his brother.

Constance stopped talking. She intently watched her uncle. There was a change in his face. "We did not do what you think! Our intention was simply to hide until it was safe."

"Sire," one of the Legionnaires spoke up after Daniel nodded his head.

"We did find the Princess's gown tangled in the briars. That is why we searched the cave."

Constance now was standing completely in front of Ian. Her intention to take part in the whipping when it occurred was very clear.

"Call the Friars," Daniel said quietly, "and get clothing for these two." Ian, deep in prayer barely heard the change in Daniel's voice.

Constance simply said, "Thank you."

Giselle arrived in the Chancellor's chamber and clothed Constance.

One of the Legionnaires obtained suitable garments from Ian's room. The two were suitably garbed when the Friars arrived.

"Bless these two for their safe return," the Chancellor requested before he cloistered himself with one of the Friars in deep remorse and confession.

For days the Legionnaires fanned out over the countryside searching for the highwaymen and the stolen horses. The rogues were skillful in staying just ahead of those hunting them. A report made to the Chancellor asked for permission to hunt until they found them. He granted it.

The party that Daniel had planned for his niece was delayed. Ian needed time to heal from the beating the Legionnaires had administered when he tried to protect Constance. She languished in her chambers waiting for the word that he was recovered. Several times, she and her uncle talked about what had happened. His remorse at the near whipping he had wanted to administer nagged at him. Friar Joseph spent long hours in prayer for and with the Chancellor.

Constance was left with the task of meeting the few important personages that came to the Throne Room. She was gracious and non-committal as to when the Chancellor would again be in attendance. There was talk among those who frequented the Royal Court. One morning, the Chancellor appeared while Constance was dealing with the simple things of the Royal Court.

Word had gotten back to him about the gossip. His sudden presence startled everyone, including Constance. She bowed in deference to him and excused herself, with his permission. He looked at the now silent attendants, couriers, pages, and the lone visitor. "I understand that there is some talk. It will stop." He sat on the royal throne after greeting the visitor who happened to be an old friend. He looked older and more tired to those who were there every day. He was. His actions of several weeks before had drained him and changed him. He had aged considerably.

Constance stopped by the room where Ian was recuperating. He was pacing the floor. Most of his cuts and bruises were faint but he had a distinct limp now. "You are not supposed to be here," he said when she entered.

"Daniel is in the Throne Room stopping the gossip," she responded. "The look on their faces when he came in." She stopped abruptly. "You are limping," concern filled her voice.

"Yes, and it doesn't seem to be getting any less."

"I am so sorry," she murmured suddenly aware that his pain and injuries had been because of her. Friar Justin had taken great pains to explain that although Ian was badly hurt, it had not been because of her disobedience, but the wounds of a warrior protecting her. Still, it hurt her to see Ian so injured.

Ian had stopped directly in front of the princess. "You are not supposed to be here." His eyes held hers.

Constance felt herself shudder since his authority over her had not diminished after the event in the cave. Her uncle had stated that, and she knew it was true. She tore her eyes away from his, and took a step backwards. "Yes, I understand," she murmured as she turned to leave.

His outreached hand stopped her. She didn't look at him. "I've missed you," he said softly. "Soon, we will be able to take walks together in the gardens." He longed for her to turn and smile at him. He released his staying hand and she quickly slipped out the door.

Once back in her own chambers, Constance flung herself on her bed and cried. She wasn't sure what she was crying about, but she knew it hurt very much. Giselle came in worried. "Go away," Constance half sobbed. Her lady did but not without a look of worry on her face.

When Constance declined the noon meal, Giselle called for Friar Justin. She was waiting for him in the greeting room when he arrived. "The princess is in distress."

"Do you know why?" the friar asked.

"No, she came up from the Throne Room and went to bed crying."

The Chancellor is in the Throne Room?"

"Do you suppose they had words?"

The friar shook his head. "From what I have heard, he has been very pleased with her manner and dealings in the Throne Room."

"Something is wrong," Giselle insisted. "She refused to eat her meal."

"She is not hungry?" Friar Justin asked both as a question and a statement. "Has she seen Ian?"

"Only when he came here to visit with her last week," Giselle tried to imagine how that would cause her charge to cry so.

"Where is she now?"

"In her bed chamber."

"Tell her I am waiting to see her in the library," then the Friar paused. "No, I will be in the Chapel and I am expecting her," he amended.

Giselle nodded as the Friar left the room.

"I don't want to go to the Chapel. Why is he asking for me? Did you tell him I did not eat and that I was crying?" Constance's excuses turned into an accusation.

Giselle's silence answered the question.

"You had no right!" The young woman screamed back.

Giselle bowed her head before she answered the girl. "When you scream like that," Giselle stopped before continuing. "I have the responsibility to help you even though you do not want me to do so."

Constance did not respond for she had heard her own ugliness when she screamed at Giselle. Her lady was correct and her uncle would confirm that with a sharp pinch if he had been present.

"All right, I will go to the Chapel," she assented. "I will need fresh water to cleanse my face."

Giselle nodded. "I will comb your hair."

"It is a bit of a tangled mess right now, like I have been tossing and turning on my bed." Constance gave a half smile. "I would like to have my hair combed."

Giselle left to obtain the basin of water and returned with another of the attendants carrying the basin and water pitcher and fresh towels.

Friar Justin stopped by the invalid Ian's room on his way back to the chapel. "Have you seen the Princess today?"

Ian eyes flickered before he answered. "Yes, Friar." He had been pleased to see the friar but with that being the opening comment, he wasn't sure.

Friar Justin then turned to ask about his recovery, his limp that he had noticed and did not bring up Constance's name. After a short chat, he gave Ian his blessing and went on his way to the Chapel.

Ian pondered the short visit in his heart.

Constance was completely refreshed when she went to the Royal Chapel. Giselle and others had pampered her. The edges of her hair were still damp.

She genuflected and looked for the Friar. At last she spotted him on the far side, reading before the statue of Mary. Cautiously she went over near him and knelt before the statue. Since the event that took place in St. Stephen's she had become closer to the Virgin Mary.

A rustle of cloth alerted Friar Justin that she was there. "Come," he said, "Let us go into the private area." The private area was a mini chapel inside the Royal Chapel where the royal family could go and not be seen by the other visitors to the larger room. Friars Justin and Joseph often used it as a confessional room with either the Chancellor or Constance.

Constance had knelt by the screen through which she could see the Tabernacle. "Come, sit over here," the friar invited. She arose and sat in the chair he had indicated. She knew by his position in the other chair that a conversation was in order. Friar Justin also used the same seating arrangement to teach Constance about her life responsibilities, and the Church.

"You went to see Ian today." Constance who had avoided looking in the friar's face, looked up.

"Yes."

"What has your uncle instructed you?"

Constance was downcast now. The momentary lightness as she had come into the chapel was no more. "I wanted to see him," she replied with her defense and not the answer to the question.

The friar waited patiently neither indicating he had not heard the answer to his question, nor that she was deliberately avoiding it.

As the seconds grew to minutes, Constance recognized that they could be sitting there until very late. She twisted in her chair once and saw no movement from the Friar. *How can he sit so still? She* questioned in her mind. She knew the answer. *Until I answer his question. And to answer his question, I will have to admit to disobedience.* She exhaled not realizing that she had been holding her breath. "I am sorry, Friar." She attempted to get around the problem.

He still did not acknowledge her words remaining very still. He had taught her well and knew that she knew what she needed to do. He began to pray silently with his head bowed.

Although Constance liked Friar Justin very much, when he took this method to deal with her, she could very well hate him. She heard in her mind the word *hate* and cringed. She had used that word only once in her acquaintance with the Friar and had received not only a long lecture but an equally long penance.

She took a long breath before speaking. "My uncle told me not to go to his room."

"Your confession?" Constance knelt and confessed her wrong doing along with some other things. Afterward, Friar Justin talked to her about keeping her word, especially to the Chancellor. He then instructed her to go to her uncle and tell him what she had done.

The girl paled. "If I don't," she whispered.

"He will hear about it anyway," Justin smiled.

"You would tell him?" she questioned.

"No, but Ian will."

Constance hung her head.

"Why?" she asked. "Ian loves me."

"That is why, because he does love you."

The tears that had come so bitterly earlier now erupted again. "It isn't fair," she lamented.

The Friar wanted to weep with her. She had tripped up herself one more time just when she thought she was making strides. He could remember times in the past when striving for a goal in his monastic training, that he had done something as innocent but forbidden as she had. He remembered the pain of correction, and the acute self-hatred as he wrestled with the correction.

Friar Justin was glad that the Legionnaire who had escorted Constance to the Royal Chapel was waiting to escort her back.

Halfway back, she stopped. "Take me to the Chancellor." The Legionnaire responded without a question.

The Chancellor had gone into the garden, seeking solace in the coolness of the late afternoon. Constance found his sitting on a bench overlooking the Angel statue. "Uncle?" she said softly as she came upon him.

Daniel looked up. "Where is your escort?"

She pointed back behind her, "Waiting for me. I asked him to keep us uninterrupted." She sat on a bench a few feet from him.

Her uncle nodded. A light breeze sprang up and the scent of the flowers wafted over them. "Why did you come?"

Constance looked down at her hands that were clinched together. "I need to tell you something."

Daniel looked at his niece. Her tension was obvious. For a moment he really didn't want to know what she was going to say. The silence grew. "Go ahead, tell me," he said with a nod watching her struggle within herself.

"I," she started then stopped. "I went to see Ian in his room today."

Her uncle raised one eyebrow. "And I have told you not to do that."

"I was disobedient," she finally managed to say the words to her uncle.

"Why are you telling me?"

"I have been to confession. Friar Justin said I must."

Daniel nodded. "You know that I love you very much?"

Constance looked away from her uncle.

"You don't know how to handle that," Daniel continued.

She nodded and turned her gaze back to her uncle. "It is something I stopped dreaming for when I was a little girl."

"Ian loves you," he said watching her reaction very closely.

She nodded again. "I know, he has told me so." She again looked off down one of the myriads of paths that ended at the angel statue.

"And you love him," her uncle stated bluntly.

Constance's head snapped back to look at her uncle while her cheeks grew a deep pink in the waning light.

"Come, let us finish this conversation inside," Daniel stood and offered her his hand.

In the distance there came riotous shouting and cheering from the far edge of the city. They both stopped to listen.

"What is it?"

The Chancellor shook his head as several Legionnaires approached them down one of the paths. "Sire, the men who have been hunting for the stolen horses have arrived!" The Legionnaire had barely paused to bow before telling the news. "They have brought back many horses."

"The dapple gray one?" the princess asked.

The noise was growing closer. Constance's hand that was resting in the crook of Daniel's arm was suddenly taken by the waiting escorting Legionnaire while The Chancellor hurried off to the Throne Room. "I want to go see," Constance started to follow.

The voice that rumbled near her ear said, "No, not until we know what is happening." She felt him restrain her.

Why not? The question buzzed through her head. *After all, until today, I have been doing very well with things in the throne room!* She was a bit amazed that she had not said the words out loud. Skillfully, the Legionnaire guided her near but not visible to what was now taking place before the Chancellor. She could hear the hooves of prancing horses echoing from the Throne Room. She remembered the day Daniel had ridden in carrying her as hostage along with seven other Legionnaires. It was both an exciting and a scary memory. Loud shouting was going on. She felt the restrain hand of her escort when she tried to move to where she could see.

Then there was silence. She heard her uncle ask how many horses did they bring back.

"Ten, Sire!" That obviously was a good number.

"Any from the Royal Household?"

"Yes, Sire!"

"And what else did you bring back?"

If Constance could have seen, she would have known what that answer would be. "Six pairs of boots! They will not be needing them."

She stood puzzled by the answer. The grin on the faces of those around her understood. She could hear the boots being ceremoniously dropped one by one on the floor of the room.

"Well done," the Chancellor said as the witnessing crowd broke into cheers.

She could hear the horses and riders leaving the throne room as the crowd eagerly dispersed for a night of celebration. It was not every day that a gang of highwaymen had been apprehended and the countryside made safe and peaceful again.

Daniel called for Constance. Almost shielding her from the pile of boots in the middle of the floor, the Legionnaire escorted her to him. "Your horse has safely returned," her uncle said to her. She curtseyed in acknowledgement. "We will talk later," he said looking at her and wondering where he was going to find a husband capable and worthy of his niece.

Constance cried again that evening when it was confirmed that her gray horse and Ian's had both been rescued. "What was the meaning of the boots?" she asked Giselle. The lady in waiting didn't answer for a long time.

Constance was beginning to think she probably wouldn't get an answer when Giselle, speaking very quietly, said, "The highwaymen are all dead."

"Oh." *Discipline, pain and justice,* she repeated in her mind. Friar Justin had been teaching her about justice and how it was often a part of discipline and pain. Her tears were that of a maturing woman, one who was beginning to understand. Giselle sat on the edge of her bed and gently rubbed her back until Constance fell asleep.

The Edge of Maturity

The distractions of the returned Legionnaires, and recovery of the horses contributed to the Chancellor's failure to continue his conversation with Constance very soon. It had been a long time since the guardians of the kingdom; mainly the Royal Legionnaires had come home with such a decisive victory. For days, impromptu parades erupted anytime several of the Legionnaires were visible as a group.

Ian was invited to reclaim his mount and ride with them as they drank in the cheers of the people. Seeing him wearing the crest on his shoulder again, and the friendly grins from the Legionnaires sent a chill up Constance's spine. A couple of those very same men had beaten Ian so badly and so unceremoniously carried her back to the castle weeks before. Ian seemed to ignore those memories.

"What do I do with my memories and feelings?" She was begging for an answer. Friar Justin had listened with his eyes closed.

"Pray for them. That is what Ian did."

Constance hung her head for she had known the answer but had hoped Friar Justin would tell her something different. She whispered, "I can't."

He returned with, "That is the only way."

One afternoon, Ian showed up at Constance's chambers and invited her to ride with him. When she hesitated, he looked at her hard. "Have you tired of me already?"

"Oh, no," she blushed. Then she paused and looked down at the floor. "I have been thinking."

Ian's eyebrows rose. "About me, I hope."   Sighing,   Constance asked. "Sidesaddle, I suppose?"

He laughed, "Oh, you still want to ride like a lad?"

"No, I mean yes." She was flustered. "My question pertains to what I wear for our ride now."

He looked at her in silence before he said, "We will be here and in the city. As the Princess, you should look like one."

"And the Legionnaires will be always at our sides?" Although she asked it as a question, there was a sharpness of a bold statement.

"You do not want to go?" he asked in reply.

"I will change and be ready quickly." she replied as she saw the possibility of being refused riding privileges by Ian.

He nodded and bowed before he left her. She stood puzzled by his formalities.

Giselle had heard some of the conversation. "Which gown do you wish to wear?" she asked when Constance finally turned.

"You were listening?" Constance accused.

"Don't I always to be ready to your every need?"

"Don't answer me in riddles!" Constance walked past her into her inner chambers. "The blue dress with the white lace at the collar and wrists," she spoke her order to her lady somewhat harshly.

Giselle and another of the ladies in waiting looked at each other. "Would you like me to help her?" the younger woman asked. Giselle nodded and turned away. She asked herself. *Were my feelings that obvious?* She hurried toward one of the back rooms and found something to do that would keep her away from her charge for a while.

Constance looked up in surprise when the other woman came into her room. "Where is Giselle?"

"Something called her away," the younger woman said as she removed the blue dress from the gown room. "Do you need me to do your hair?"

With the help of the younger woman, Constance was ready for riding in a very short period of time. "Send for my escort."

The woman bowed and went to the entry room where she found a Legionnaire already there in waiting. She curtseyed. "She is nearly ready."

Ian sat upon his horse that had been stolen, loosely holding the reins to the big gray, thinking about the attitude he had observed in Constance. It was good that they were going to ride with an escort through-out the city. The town's people could not get their fill of seeing their beloved Royal Legionnaires riding about. When the Chancellor suggested adding the Princess to the mix, Ian had been happy to have her ride beside him again. They had been apart for much too long. He missed her and he had thought she was missing him but after the comments in her chambers, he wasn't too certain about that now.

The Chancellor was busy in the Royal Court with some legal problems. His dear old friend, Frederick, visited him frequently. The casual watchers in the Royal Court had noticed the man's coming and going a lot. The two men often went to the King's private chambers to discuss their common topic, the future marriage of Constance.

This was one of those days when summer was nearly over and the hint of autumn was in the air. The crops had been abundant so the marketplace was busy. Red apples, late summer vegetables, and assorted early fall produce crowded the stalls.

The atmosphere in the city was heady with expectation that all was well with their kingdom. The daily tours made by the Royal Legionnaires, although frequent, did not bore them. They were ever ready to stop what they were doing to watch a group ride by. The excitement grew when that day when the touring Legionnaires were escorting the Princess Constance. Children ran alongside frighteningly close to the hoof's horses of the contingent as they wove their way through the crowded streets.

At first Constance had been dismayed at the masses yelling, cheering, and waving as Ian escorted her with the constant Legionnaires keeping the crowds back from them. Winding through the narrower streets, she could almost touch the walls of the buildings. They then turned on to the broad boulevard that ended at the plaza where the Blessed Be God Cathedral stood. Constance drank in the beauty of the city and its people in her impromptu ride. She was glad that she had chosen the blue gown with the lace at the collar and wrists. It showed off her fairness while accenting her blossoming maturity.

No one watched her as closely as Ian. He had been stunned when she had arrived at the stable so maturely dressed. The little disagreement they had had before the ride was forgotten as he realized that soon she would be Queen. His companion, the woman he had protected, although poorly he thought, in the cave. The woman who had in return protected him from certain death at the hands of the Chancellor, Constance, whom he loved, was truly a royal woman.

Six Legionnaires, Ian and Constance broke away from the others and left the city proper. The ride through the countryside was exhilarating for Constance. Here and there, people come out of the small houses to wave and watch the unplanned event. A fast gallop through a pristine meadow brought them back to the castle.

Giselle looked at the bright flush of excitement on the cheeks of her charge and smiled. "It was a good ride?" She asked as she helped her undress.

"Yes," Constance nodded. "There were so many people!"

"And Ian?" Giselle said as she began to brush out some of the windblown in tangles from Constance's hair.

"Ouch," the girl complained as Giselle was combing her snarled hair.

"Your uncle wants you to have dinner with him this evening, and it will never do for you to go with these tangles."

"Uncle Daniel?"

"You have another uncle?" Giselle answered as the comb now smoothly slid through her hair.

"No, but he hasn't spoken to me for weeks."

"He has been busy, my child." Giselle had told her that many times after her interrupted talk with her uncle in the Royal Gardens when the Legionnaires had returned with the horses.

She sighed, "Yes, I know. That is always what you say." She pulled away quickly.

Giselle did not let go of her hair. "If you don't stand still," Giselle threatened.

Laughing, Constance yielded. "What are you going to do, pinch me?"

There was silence in the room when Giselle did nothing but stand and stare at her charge. She let Constance put on her own dress, only aiding with the buttons on the sleeves.

Constance was uncomfortable with the silence but stubborn enough not to be the one to break it.

Giselle pointed to the Crucifix on the wall. Constance turned her head away as Giselle left the room. She was dressed too formally to just throw herself on the bed in a tantrum. She bolted out the door of her chambers in her blind rage. The ever-present Legionnaire took up stride as she rushed through the corridors toward the Royal Chapel She only slowed when the accompanying Legionnaire restrained her by placing her hand in the proper position on his arm. At the chapel door, she shook off his restraint and opened the door herself and closed it behind her. The chapel appeared empty. Only a few candles were lit. She threw herself down at the foot of the statue of the Virgin Mary and wailed, softly she thought.

"Sssh" a voice whispered near her. She knew who had spoken. Friar Justin was sitting in contemplation a short distance away.

"It is not fair," she savagely whispered her reply.

"Probably not," the Friar answered. "But your behavior is not either."

"How do you know?" she challenged back.

"Be still," his voice commanded with authority.

She complied only because of previous long lessons in silence upon her knees administered by the Friar.

After what seemed like a very long time, the Friar stood and said, "Let us retire to the other room."

Constance followed him obediently.

"What isn't fair?" He pointed to one chair and took another.

Constance looked at him blankly having forgotten she had said that earlier.

He didn't offer her any clues.

She buried her face in her hands as the growing awareness of her behavior when she had spoken to Giselle and later to him had been childish. The tears that flowed were repented tears.

The Friar consented to hear her confession. On the outside of the Chapel the Legionnaire tried to explain to the courier from the Chancellor that the princess was inside and not wanting to be disturbed.

"The Chancellor expects her for dinner," the frustrated courier stated for the second time. When he moved to open the door, the Legionnaire rested his own hand on his sheathed sword. "What do I tell him, the courier pleaded?

"She is with the Friar," answered the Legionnaire hoping that there was some truth in the statement.

The courier scurried away, terrified with his failure to fetch the Princess. He repeated over and over to himself, 'she is with the Friar', so as not to forget in his fright when it was evident that he had not brought the Princess back with him.

When she emerged later, the Legionnaire told her of the courier and the dinner she was supposed to have with the Chancellor. She nodded and allowed him to escort her to the Chancellor's private quarters.

Daniel had received the information from his frightened courier rather calmly especially when he learned that she was in the Royal Chapel and with the Friar. "The Princess Constance," the doorkeeper announced when she arrived.

"Sire," Constance curtseyed.

When the door had closed behind her, he softly said, "You look lovely, my dear."

"Thank you, Sire."

"Uncle Daniel," he replied.

She inclined her head.

"I thought we would have dinner together and continue where we were talking when we were interrupted several weeks ago. Interesting that you have just come from being with the Friar. If I remember right," he paused with a smile, "you had been with him just before you found me in the garden. I hope you don't have to tell me something."

Constance thought a minute before she remembered what she had said to him in the garden. "No, Uncle."

"Good," he said as he pulled out the chair at the table for her to sit.

After the meal, they sat near the small fireplace and watched the wood burn. "I always like sitting and watching a fire." Daniel seemed to be in a reminiscent mood. "It reminds me of some peaceful times when I was a child before life became so complicated. Watch that log when it begins to break into two pieces from the fire."

Constance sat in silence as together they listened to the fire pop and crackle until a stronger cracking sound was heard as the log began to break. One end dropped down out of the range of the flames, while the other leaned over the hot bed of coals and continued to be consumed by the fire.

Daniel sighed. "That one is me," he said pointing to the piece that was out of the range of the flames.

She looked at him puzzled.

"The one burning bright, full of light and heat is you." Again, he sighed. "It always happens that way when the time comes to change from one leader to another."

"No!"

If Daniel was surprised at her response, he did not indicate it. "Forever a child, it cannot be," he looked at her pale face.

She nodded for she knew that was true. The weeks she had spent in the Royal Court while Daniel was unable had shown her a picture of her future life.

"And the good princess needs a husband to whom she can turn when life in the Royal Court is boring. Of course, she will be the Queen then." He was watching her out of the corner of his eye. She had not moved. *Bless the Friar who has stilled her restlessness and helped her mature. I shall be indebted to him forever.*

Constance moved in her chair. "Uncle?"

He turned to look straight at her.

"You have found someone to be a husband for me?" *I know it isn't Ian because both have explained to me why that would not be acceptable.* "Is it someone I already have met?"

"Ian?" he asked to test the ground.

"No," she said, "Someone who has visited the Royal Court."

"No, I do not know who he is yet. There is many vying for a royal bid, but the one for you, probably doesn't even know of you yet."

"Oh," she said. "Will I get to know him before we are promised?"

Daniel nodded his head. "You both will have a say, if that will help ease your concerns."

Constance nodded. "What do I do with Ian?"

"Find a place for him in your service. A lad of his intelligence is not very common and his love and concern for you will make him an asset."

"Will he still be my companion for a while until . . ." She let her voice and thoughts trail off.

"Yes, a more devoted and loyal servant you will not find."

"He says he loves me," Constance was now looking earnestly into her uncle's face.

"I know, and you love him."

She ducked her head not wanting Daniel to see the truth in her eyes even though he had just told it to her.

"My good friend, Frederick is traveling for me, for you. He is letting other royal households know of your eligibility. Yours is different than most because your husband will have to come here rather than you going there. That will make the selection easier."

Constance just nodded. She had not thought of marriage as part of being the Queen. Obviously, if there were to be heirs, she would have to be married. This thought frightened her more than the one of being Queen someday. Someday was becoming very close.

The last of the flaming wood had burned to ashes. "It is late, go to your chambers and thank God for the man that will be your husband." Daniel had stood. He escorted Constance to the door and before he opened it, he embraced her within gentleness but firmness. "Do not be afraid, my child, you will be loved by whomever he is."

Interlude

Month's passed with no mention of marriage to Constance although she was aware of Daniel's friend Frederick coming and going at various times. When the weather was acceptable, she and Ian rode their horses, sometimes in the close by meadows but at other times they ventured into the woods and on further. They visited the entrance of the cave they had taken shelter in and discussed the fear, pain, and consequence events of that adventure.

"And I wasn't even trying to run away," Constance laughed when she told of him her first adventure at the briars and cave. She neglected to tell Ian that was where Daniel first began to discipline her. It was still too private a memory to be shared even with her best friend, Ian.

Ian talked about his family in the mountains, watching the flocks and his first scary night of watching the flock in the dark and alone with only the family herd dog as his companion. He talked about his sisters and their families.

"Have you ever been back to visit them?" Constance asked.

Ian looked at her quizzically. "I have never thought of doing that since I entered the service of the Royal Court. I pretty much expected that I would never return to them when the Page Master paid them a small fee for me."

"You are a purchased servant?" Constance was shocked. "That is nothing more than a slave."

"My family had a need for the money and saw it as a way for me not to be just a tender of the flocks for all of my life."

"But you serve under my uncle Daniel directly now. Are you still a purchased servant?"

"I don't know," Ian admitted. "I have spoken with the Chancellor about being a member of the Royal Legion and I have had some training with them."

"The men who nearly killed you?" she asked in dismay.

"No, but they did hurt me." He smiled. "If I remember correctly, you are the one who kept the Chancellor from killing me."

Constance blushed. They had turned their horses toward the castle. "You would have given your life for me, it seemed that was the least I could do for you." She urged her horse into a trot.

Ian caught up quickly and took hold of her reins bringing her horse to a halt. "But you didn't have to," he said looking deep into her eyes. She tried to look away. He used his riding crop to gently turn her head back toward him.

Constance shivered from his intimate closeness and authority over her. "Our lives are going to change," she said softly.

He had withdrawn his crop from the edge of her face. He had seen the closeness of tears in her eyes. "I know," he responded gently.

"My uncle is looking for a husband for me." They had talked about this before but it had never seemed so life changing until now.

"He has found someone?"

She shrugged her shoulders. "I don't know. Frederick comes and goes but no one is telling me anything. I have lessons daily with the Friars and they aren't telling me anything either."

"Do you ask them?" Ian watched her face contort with emotions.

"No, they told me that information was the Chancellor's privilege to speak only."

"They are correct in that," Ian inserted.

"Can we ride back to the castle now?" Constance was looking straight into his eyes. "I think I want to be alone." The pang of sadness that swept over Ian left him feeling numb. He handed her reins back and together the returned to the castle. She left him without a word after he had helped her dismount.

She knew if she returned to her private rooms, she would only be a worry to Giselle so she accepted her Legionnaire escort and told him to take her to the chapel. Once there, in secrecy at the feet of the Virgin Mary statue, she wept. Friar Joseph found her there when he returned after a long talk with the Chancellor. Friar Justin was now the prefect of St. Stephen's Monastery. It was in moments like this that Friar Joseph missed him. He had a way of cutting through Constance's pain and emotions that he, Joseph, did not have. He could only wait until she was aware of him or looked at him. For him to speak out otherwise was not of his nature or bearing.

Constance was aware of the Friar's presence. She debated about speaking to him or just getting up and leaving. After many minutes of indecision, she rose and looked to the Friar. "I am afraid," she said as she had said to him the first time she was with him.

Friar Joseph nodded. "Does the Blessed Mother know of your fear? I am sure she had a few herself."

Constance smiled and sat down in the pew across the aisle from where he sat. "She must be tired of hearing me complain."

"And her response?"

Constance dropped her head in shame. "Peace, my daughter, peace."

"Why are you ashamed?"

The quickness that the Princess looked up told him that she had not even considered herself ashamed. "I am not," she stated firmly.

"Then why the downcast face?"

"I do not know."

"What has Friar Justin spoken to you about truthfulness?"

She really wanted to get up and leave. The conversation was too close to where she hurt. Manners were something else that Friar Justin had also taught her. His shadowed presence was in the chapel with them. "I am sorry, Friar Joseph. My desire is not to talk about what causes me so much pain right now."

He nodded. "Then I shall pray for you and this mysterious pain."

It was her turn to nod now. "Thank you, Friar." She bowed her head and listened to the Friar pray, joining in on the Lord's Prayer.

"You had a visitor while you were out," Giselle told her when she returned to her chambers.

"Oh," Constance had not been expecting anyone.

"Your cousin from the kingdom to the south," continued her lady. "She said she would see you later in the evening when I told her you were out riding."

"The one who gave me my first hairpin?" Constance asked.

"Yes."

"I did not know she or they were expected."

"She indicated that she came by boat."

"Oh," Constance felt confused.

"Send a courier to her and ask her to come to my chambers."

"She said something about dinner with the Chancellor at this evening."

The rest of the late afternoon and evening, Constance concentrated on preparing herself for dinner with the Chancellor and their cousin. A courier came by with a formal invitation for the late dinner in the Royal Chambers.

Daniel had given her more hairpins, some studded with diamonds and others with different precious jewels. She liked putting them in her dark chestnut colored hair but for tonight decided to wear just the one her cousin had given her.

The Chancellor was confounded when Lady Rachel, his cousin, arrived alone and unannounced. "Where is the rest of the family?"

There has been trouble," Rachel replied. "I was sent away so that no harm would come to me."

"And Felix?"

"I do not know his whereabouts," She hesitated being careful not to actually say that he was probably dead.

"Do you need sanctuary?"

Rachel blushed in spite of herself.

Daniel read her face. "I am sorry for your loss. You are welcome in my house."

His cousin closed her eyes in hopes of staying the tears that wanted to rush forth. "Thank you, my Lord." As she regained her composure, she continued. "I do not wish to be a burden to you."

"You aren't," Daniel replied. "You are the answer to a prayer."

Rachel raised her eyes to her cousin's face. "How can that be?"

Daniel laughed. "Just yesterday, the Friar here in the castle had spoken to me about the need for a mature woman to help guide the Princess as she prepares for marriage and assuming the throne."

"Her lady is mature."

"Yes, but her lady is growing old. She has not the experience that you can give Constance."

"The Friar, will he hear my confession?"

Daniel nodded thinking of the hours of confession and counsel that the Friars had devoted to him.

It was on the way to the Royal Chapel that Rachel had stopped by Constance's Chambers while the young woman had been still out riding.

The two women met over dinner with Daniel. Each had been delighted to see the other. Rachel noticed that Constance wore the diamond-studded hairpin that she had given her years before. Constance blushed when the older woman complimented her.

"Uncle Daniel has given me several more pins. I wore yours in honor of you tonight." The maturing princess said gracefully. "It is still my favorite."

As they ate together the story of why Rachel had come slowly came out. Constance cried when she realized that her second cousin was a widow now. Daniel, also discomforted by the tragedy that had befallen his cousin, watch how Rachel affected Constance. He saw anew the maturity that his niece was developing.

"I want your Aunt Rachel to instruct you now. She will have her own private chambers near you. Giselle will continue to manage the ladies in your chamber still."

The announcements, instructions and proclamation of her Aunt Rachel's position over Constance seemed smothering. She thought she was finally beginning to be able to express herself and show her maturity. Her face must have given her away.

"Oh, my dear," Rachel said turning to her as though Daniel was not in the room. "This is a time of blooming, and a preparation for your queenship. You need the counsel of a trusted older woman who understands much of what will be expected of you. You need a confidant and a loyal friend."

Constance dabbed at her eyes with her napkin. "It is so overwhelming."

Rachel glanced at Daniel who had stood. He understood the silent communication and left the room.

"If your mother had lived, or even Daniel's wife, you would have had that all these years." Rachel cautiously placed her arm around Constance.

The girl readily leaned into the comforting arm and sobbed. "I have been so lonely," she whispered. "Does that make sense?"

Rachel nodded as she felt her own tears fall down her face. "Absolutely."

After Constance, accompanied by Rachel, had gone back to her chamber, Daniel paced the floor. He had not expected such a tender and heartrending evening. In some ways he was done with the upbringing of his niece. It made him feel terribly old. *But then*, he mused to himself, *I still have to find her a suitable husband.* He wondered what his cousin Rachel was thinking. She really needed comforted, or did she? Women always seemed to find a channel when things were difficult.

He remembered his mother as she realized his father was dying, and with his death his younger brother was going to claim the throne. She had gone to the monastery to stay after the King died and she never looked back. Her heart was broken by her husband's death, and then the atrocities committed by her younger son in his usurping of the throne from the rightful heir. She had died in less than a year praying for the souls of her sons, one a murderer, the other, accused of murder.

Daniel remembered his last conversation with his mother, speaking through the grill that separated those cloistered, where she had sought refuge, from the rest of the world. They whispered to each other for now he was being sought for a murder he did not commit, and she only spoke in whispers now. He wept.

Lady Rachel

*T*he days passed quickly after Rachel came to stay at the castle. Constance was at a loss as how to relate to this new woman. She realized that her great aunt knew a lot about how the kingdom functioned. Rachel knew what would be expected from the young princess when she assumed the throne. Also, Rachel liked to ride as much as she did.

Her lessons were concentrated in the mornings first with the Friar and then with Rachel. If the activity in the court was light, they spent the afternoons doing 'girl things'. When they rode with their constant Royal Legionnaires nearby, Ian often joined them. They laughed at the same things and seemed to weep in unison.

Rachel told Constance about her last days with her husband as their country erupted with a revolution that started among the more lawless people then spread into the villages and towns and finally to the royal castle there. "Although we did not participate with the Royal Family, the Revolutionaries decided all royalty must die. For days, we hid as the Revolutionaries searched the royal household and even broke into the places of safety such as the monasteries and the churches. My husband, Felix, promising to follow the next day sought out a foreign boat captain who spirited me onto his boat. When many of the boats in the harbor were being torched, the captain set sail without him. Word had gotten to the harbor that all the royalists were dead."

For a long time, Constance was silent as she stared at some indistinct plant in the Royal Gardens. "Were you able to bring anything with you?" She already knew that the seamstress was busy making new gowns for her great aunt.

"What I had; I paid the captain to take me here. This was not where he was going at first. I gave him my jeweled hairpins, a cameo that Felix had given me, and my rings. He was satisfied and honored his word to Felix to see that I got safely here."

Constance had noticed that Rachel had not worn any hairpins since her arrival and had wondered why. Her imagination had thought of many reasons, but not the one that Rachel just told her. She touched her hair and thought about how much Rachel's gift several years ago had impressed her. "You may have some of mine," she said.

"I don't need hairpins now," Rachel smiled. 'I am just a pauper relative living here thanks to Daniel. "It would seem uncouth for me to flaunt any wealth."

"Even if I gave them to you as a gift?"

"Yes," Rachel answered as she looked away hoping to hide the pain in her eyes.

Neither spoke for a time, as each was lost in painful memories and thoughts.

"Frederick is here," Constance murmured into the silence.

Rachel already knew that for he had brought her such distressing news the evening before. "Yes, he confirmed Felix's death."

Constance looked up into the face of her great aunt. "Oh! Why did you not tell me right away?"

"You are still a child," Rachel replied thinking that she had wanted to protect Constance from life and death.

It had been months since Constance had felt the intense anger of being called a child. It took her by surprise. "I am not a child," she said curtly and stood. She wanted to flee from the garden, maybe even run away.

Surprised, Rachel's mouth was hanging open. "I did not want to upset you needlessly. I have suspected that what the ship's captain told me was true."

Constance now stood with her back to the woman. The hovering Legionnaires who were keeping watch had seen Constance's move. One stepped forward. Constance heard his footstep on the stony path. Without looking back at Rachel, she spoke to him. "I want to go inside now." He offered her his arm and they walked away together.

Rachel had bowed her head as the tears flowed down her face. The remaining Legionnaire stepped to her side. She waved him away as for a short time she cried for the loss of her husband. She had not shed any tears over him until then.

"Did the Lady insult you?" the quiet growl from the man escorting her cut into Constance's thoughts.

She knew the growl. He had been with her many a time when her behavior was not correct. She stopped walking. "No, she did not insult me," She had not realized that her thought was verbalized until she felt the harder than normal tug for her to keep walking. As she mused on the previous conversation in the garden, she was unaware of where she was until the Legionnaire had stopped, bowed low and opened the door to the Royal Chapel. A flash of insight almost overwhelmed her. She had been rude to the Lady Rachel!

She knelt in shame and sorrow. *What will Daniel say?* She did not like the thought of telling her uncle how she had behaved. *Will Rachel tell him?* She hoped not.

Giselle was disturbed when Rachel sent a courier asking for Constance. She thought the two were together. She sent for Ian. That messenger found him in the stables. It was growing late, *where was Constance?* It did not take Giselle's worry long before all the ladies-in-waiting in the Princess's chamber were worried also. Ian arrived after changing clothing. He had been helping groom some of the horses and he still had the lingering odor of stable on him.

"Have you seen her," Giselle asked.

"No," Ian answered with the customary bow. "I thought she and Rachel were going to spend the afternoon in the Royal Garden."

"Rachel just sent a courier asking for Constance."

"Shall I go look for her?"

Giselle nodded for by now she was numb with worry.

Ian looked for the two Legionnaires who had been the aunt and niece's escorts. He only found the one who had been with Rachel. "Where would he," referring to the other Legionnaire, "have taken her?" There was a shake of the head and a worried scowl on the face of the man. Together, they began a search for the missing man and Constance.

It had been a long day in the Royal Court plus the sad news brought back by Frederick about Rachel's husband. The Chancellor was lingering at the edge of the Royal Garden when Ian and the Legionnaire approached. "Have you seen Constance?" Ian blurted out as he bowed before the Chancellor.

Alarm and fear sprang onto Daniel's face. "Where is her escort?" He was looking straight at the other Legionnaire.

"He left the garden with her, Sire."

"Find him!" Daniel's thoughts were on the malcontent that was simmering in the kingdom where his cousin had lived. Anytime one kingdom was affected, it often showed up in the others. It was like a sickness spreading sometimes like wildfire. There were those in his kingdom who would know of the revolutionary events happening elsewhere sometimes seeming to be known without any contact between the kingdoms. Only, he knew that there was as Frederick had told him.

Near the door of the Chapel, the gruff voiced Legionnaire was patiently waiting for the Princess. Inside, unaware of the turmoil that was erupting in key spots of the castle, Constance was still on her knees. She had cried for a little while but knew that would not solve her problem.

She heard the door open and shut. She hoped it was the Friar. When she looked up, Ian was standing in front of her. He asked, "Where have you been?"

Outside, the two Legionnaires were nose to nose in a not so friendly conversation. "Where is the Princess?"

Since Ian had gone into the Chapel, the gruff voiced Legionnaire was at a loss as what the question meant. "She has been in there since leaving the Royal garden." he replied keeping a wary eye on the other Legionnaire sensing that he might attack him.

"They are looking all over the castle for her. And you!"

Although Ian was glad to find her, his hard look scared her. "I've done nothing wrong," she said in her defense wondering why he seemed so angry.

"Tell that to the Chancellor," he answered back barely moving his lips, his countenance was severe.

There was a scuffling sound just outside the Chapel door before it opened. The two Legionnaires entered, apparently in disagreement. Constance was standing now. She looked to Ian and then to the other two men.

"Cease your activities," a voice interrupted the tenseness of the moment. Friar Joseph came into the chapel. "What is going on? This chapel is the same as a church."

The Legionnaires ceased their grappling with each other. Constance moved away from Ian toward the Friar. "I have been praying in here for some time. That man," she pointed to the one with the gruff voice, "is my escort and has been waiting outside for me."

The Friar looked toward Ian. "I was sent to find the Princess. She has been missing."

"Well, you found me, so I am no longer missing." At this moment, Constance was nearly as angry as she had been in the garden. "Friar, explain to these men," she indicated Ian and the other Legionnaire, "that I often spend time here in the Royal Chapel!"

Friar Joseph looked at each one separately lingering for at least a minute before looking to the next. When his eyes met Constance's eyes she dropped her defiant gaze. Ian dropped to his knees, as did the two Legionnaires. They each had a deep respect for the religious and they were ashamed of their behavior that he had seen when he walked in.

"I will hear your confessions when you are ready," Friar Joseph said mildly.

"What about the Chancellor?" Ian burst out with. "He still thinks she is missing."

"I will hear his also if he is at the bottom of this fracas." The Friar moved toward the Confessional. He looked at Constance just before he entered and closed the door behind him.

Constance had read his eyes clearly. He wanted her to respond first. She did not disappoint him as she knelt on the other side of the screen.

Two chastened Legionnaires, unused to kneeling before a Friar, escorted Constance to Daniel's chambers. Ian spread the word that it was just a misunderstanding as the Princess often spends time in the Royal Chapel.

Daniel looked worried and tired when she stepped into his private rooms after being announced. He listened to her explanation of her guilt of rudeness to Lady Rachel in silence. "I am sorry," she said.

"What about your disappearance?"

"I was in the Royal Chapel praying. My escort was there with me. Is it wrong for me to be there?"

"No, it is the right place to be when you have sinned." Daniel sighed. "Apologize to Lady Rachel."

"I shall," she answered and then she said, "Uncle, did you really think I had done something so awful and had run away?

"I was praying to God that you hadn't." Daniel stepped toward her. He saw her cringe although she hid it well. "I love you, Constance." He put his arms around her and hugged her close. They both fought back tears.

Jolcum

The days and weeks passed quickly. Several times a month, a candidate for Constance's hand in marriage would make his presence known. There would be formalities in the Royal Court, gifts displayed, the inevitable banquet and tedious interview with the Chancellor Daniel, and gracious teas with the Princess and her Lady Rachel. Frederick frequented the castle, more often to talk with Daniel but sometimes to speak privately with Constance. His counsel to her was to learn from the various meetings, not to look at the gifts as something she deserved, and to wait.

Friar Joseph was as annoying as the many visitors with his constant reminders of what a Godly husband would be like. It was late summer and no visitors were expected. Constance proposed to Lady Rachel that they go riding. A full contingent of Royal Legionnaires was assigned to secure the surrounding area as Ian, Constance, Rachel and the two constant Legionnaire escorts set off for a ride, a picnic and maybe a time alone. Ian rode ahead of the women to allow them to converse freely while the other two men rode within sight but out of hearing of the ladies.

"I am feeling like I am going to war," Constance commented to her friend. "All the bother just for a private ride is so amusing."

Lady Rachel smiled. "You are a valuable personage now, my dear Constance."

"Future queen and all that stuff," Constance tossed off lightly.

"And it is known far and wide that you are nearing eligibility for marriage."

The future queen shrugged her shoulders. "You would think the kingdom is at stake."

Lady Rachel reined her horse. "It is," she said softly as Constance drew her horse up beside her.

Constance sat looking off to where Ian was ahead of her. "He would have made a good husband." They had talked about this several times.

A strange bird whistle had been sounded by the Legionnaires behind bringing Ian to a halt. He turned in his saddle and saw the women talking. He waited patiently until they once again urged their horses to a fast walk. He wondered what had been so important to Constance or Lady Rachel to stop. He did not know it was a private discussion about him.

"I know, he is not of royal blood, but he is of royal blood, the blood of Christ." Constance was arguing the point that never went anywhere, with her uncle, Giselle, Lady Rachel or the Friar. She sighed. Then as if a sudden insight struck her, she asked. "Why did my uncle allow us to become so close?"

Rachel looked at her for a long time. "Maybe he didn't realize what would happen."

"Don't let Uncle Daniel hear you say that," Constance replied. "I brought that up once and I thought he was going to beat me!"

"That is one of the oddities of men," Rachel nodded. "When they are confronted with a piece of truth that you thought they should have known, they react."

"Felix did?"

"Not very often. I quickly learned what not to confront him on." Rachel's smile seemed a bit sad. "I miss him so."

"I am sorry I have made you sad by mentioning him," Constance apologized.

"Ian's waiting, I suppose we should continue our ride," Rachel did not acknowledge the pain and sadness she felt.

About midday they were in a beautiful meadow, somewhat near the cave. Seeing no encroaching briars, they stopped and spread out their picnic in the shade of a large tree. Ian joined them as the Legionnaires tended the horses and sat nearby.

From the woods a pair of human eyes was watching. The figure had escaped detection first by the contingency of Legionnaires, and now by those in the small riding group. He sat in the crook of another large tree silently calculating his next move. His own personal group was keeping just far enough ahead of the contingency and being sighted by them to allow for a sense of safety for the Royal riders.

Jolcum was the man's name. He had been to the court bringing gifts for the Princess and leaving when he had not been even greeted by her. One might have described him as a jilted suitor although no one was promised anything when they visited the Chancellor and the Royal Court.

Ian had seen movement in the upper branches of the large tree where Jolcum was. Rather than sounding an alarm, he encouraged the women to pack up what remained of their picnic and go to their mounts. The two did as he said although surprised at the sharpness of his order. Ian kept behind the women until they were mounted and then spoke to the Legionnaires about what he had seen.

As Ian and the women began to continue their ride, the Legionnaires held back and circled around. Jolcum decided to remain in the tree until he was sure there were no more lingering outriders. He was surprised when a voice called up from the foot of the tree he was in, "Do you wish to ride or walk?" One Legionnaire with sword drawn was standing at the base of the tree. He glanced to where that Legionnaire indicated and saw another with bow drawn.

"I will come down," he replied.

"Drop your sword by the hilt."

He did know the one with the bow could pierce his light amour with an arrow before he had an opportunity to defend himself.

"Come down," the one below him called.

Jolcum wore the crest of his kingdom. He hoped that these brutes would honor that when he got to the ground. He dropped the last few feet to the spongy soil under the mature tree.

"Who are you?"

"Jolcum of ...." He didn't get to finish his words before the nearest Legionnaire struck him.

"What were you doing spying on Princess Constance?"

Cautiously rising up from the ground where the unexpected blow had left him, he bowed before attempting to speak. "I was not spying on the Princess."

"Don't lie to us," the second Legionnaire was now within striking distance of Jolcum. "You were in the Royal Court just a few days ago. You do not honor your crest. You were bid to depart."

Jolcum bowed again keeping his eyes open hoping to avoid another blow. "I did leave but my heart was smitten."

"With the Princess, you barely saw her?"

"No, I am much too old for her. It was of her Lady that I was smitten."

"So, you waited hoping to speak with Lady Rachel?" The Legionnaires found the idea incredulous and laughed.

"She is a widow, I have lost my wife," Jolcum said softly judging the distance between the two men and wondering how many more were hiding in the woods just waiting for him to do something dumb.

"You can tell it to the Chancellor," the Legionnaire with the gruff voice stated. "Where is your mount?"

"In the gully over there," Jolcum pointed. He realized he would have difficulty in calling for his horse with the way his mouth was swelling from the earlier blow.

"Call him." Jolcum made an attempt to whistle for his steed. It apparently was close enough to his normal whistle for the horse answered with a low snort. They could hear the horse struggling to climb directly up the side of the gully.

"Go get him," the Legionnaire with the bow and arrow ordered his counterpart. He held the arrow straight at Jolcum's heart.

A few minutes later, the horse was led from the shallow end of the gully up to the two waiting on top. Jolcum was glad he had sent his entourage ahead and kept no one with him for surely the one with the bow would have put the arrow through his heart in an instance if there had been any scuffle.

When they started to bind his hands behind him after he was mounted, he said, "I am from the bloodline of my king. May my word be my binding?"

Reluctantly, the one Legionnaire nodded. "Bind his hands in front of him," he ordered the other.

They then turned back toward the castle, signaling with the bird whistle for other Legionnaires to join them. Ian heard the signal and relaxed a little. He turned back toward the castle with the two women.

"Why are you cutting our ride short?" Constance called out to him as she brought her horse to a standstill. Other bird whistles sounded in the distance. Ian understood their message.

Lady Rachel, vaguely aware of the whistles, turned her horse back and then saw Constance sitting on her horse and staring at Ian. "Come on Constance, it is nearly time to head back anyway," she tried to reason with the Princess.

Ian moved his horse in close to Constance. He noted the tightness of her mouth. "Because I gave the order," he said in a quiet voice. She lifted her hand holding her reins to urge the horse to move. Lady Rachel, a short distance away saw the riding crop in Ian's hand raise but did not hear it strike. He laid it gently across Constance's arm as he took her reins.

She sat immobile glaring at Ian. Her breath came in short spurts. Constance was speechless.

"If I have to raise it again," Ian paused, looking his Princess and dear friend hard in the eyes, "it will not come down softly."

She blinked to hold back the tears that wanted to come. She nodded and let him lead her horse beside his for a while. She was overcome with shame. She wondered what Lady Rachel thought. She had seen the deep love in Ian's eyes just before he had chastened her. It was hard for her to cry as he moved the horses into a trot. Safely sitting sidesaddle became the major challenge.

Lady Rachel had swung her right leg over the saddle to safely continue at the pace that Ian set. "Let me ride like a lad," Constance managed to get out when they had slowed for tangled brush.

Ian nodded as Constance got her right leg over the horse. It was difficult without a stirrup for the right foot but the two women more confidently kept up the pace that Ian started until several Royal Legionnaires joined them. Now surrounded by protection, the whole group moved at a fast walk for the castle.

The commotion at the castle startled the women. Something had happened and it wasn't until much later that they realized they had been in the middle of something happening. Both rode sidesaddle after the

Legionnaires had joined them. They were hurried to their individual chambers and the Legionnaires stood guard.

Ian fell on his knees in the Royal Chapel at the feet of the surprised Friar and cried out his misgiving of how he had treated the Princess. When he told the saintly Friar that he had threatened to actually cause her physical pain, the Friar grieved with him. "It is in God's providence," the Friar finally counseled and wondered how Constance was handling the emotional pain.

Until her cousin Daniel sent for her, Rachel could not learn what all the excitement was in the Royal Court. "Jolcum has returned!" was the curt answer she got from the courier as she made her way to the Throne Room. Daniel was sitting on the throne. Before him knelt Jolcum, in submission to the Chancellor's authority.

Lady Rachel was announced and she entered and curtseyed. "My Lord," she murmured as that was all she could think to say. Daniel looked at his cousin and down at the submissive Jolcum, a man who had come seeking the Princess' hand. He ordered the Throne Room cleared of all but himself, Jolcum and Rachel, and the attending guards.

"My dear cousin," Daniel spoke to her solemnly. "You came to me widowed and destitute months ago and I accepted you into my house freely. I gave you a position of honor serving the Princess Constance. You have been faithful in your counsel and guidance to her. Soon, in a year or less, Constance will be married and will also begin her reign as Queen over this kingdom."

Rachel stood mute wondering what her cousin was going to say next.

"Jolcum has asked me for your hand."

The Throne Room seemed to swirl about her in slow motion. She staggered. Someone placed a chair behind her urging her to sit. She did.

"Let it be done as you say," she managed to murmur.

Daniel ordered that what had taken place not be spoken of anywhere before he retired to his private chambers with Jolcum and Rachel.

Jolcum found himself shaking, from the encounter with the Chancellor but even more so from the submission of Rachel to her cousin's request.

The three of them talked for some time. Mostly, Daniel and Jolcum talked while Rachel listened. "You will not marry her until the Princess is wed. Rachel is much needed by the Princess."

Jolcum nodded. He understood the complexities of a royal household even if, like Rachel, he was a cousin twice removed.

Daniel turned to Rachel. "Jolcum has placed his fidelity to me and thus to the future queen. You both will remain in this kingdom."

Jolcum thought of those first tense moments before the Chancellor when his life was at stake until he was finally allowed to state his case. Daniel had made him a freed man in return for his pledge of fidelity. He had ripped the crest he wore on his shoulder off with the help of the sword of one of the Legionnaires before prostrating himself in submission.

Rachel made a detour by Constance's chamber on the way back to her own. The look on her face worried Constance until Rachel stepped in the inner sleeping room where they could talk in private.

"What is it?" Constance urged her aunt to speak.

"Daniel has pledged me to be married after you are married."

The younger woman stood amazed and silent. Finally, she said, "Who is he?"

Her aunt laughed, "Someone who came about you but was much too old for you."

"Is he old for you?"

"I do not know," she laughed, "I just met him."

"What does he look like," Constance was still young and looked to the surface and not what was in the heart.

"A good man, from what I can tell. A widower so he is older." She smiled. "He risked his life to ask Daniel for me. That is important."

"Will he be faithful?" Constance was remembering some of the traits that the Friar constantly was telling her.

"He pledged his fidelity to Daniel and the future Queen."

Constance remembered her own battle with a pledge of fidelity. "Oh."

The two women embraced. "I would think that now that my future is out of the way, yours will settle soon." Lady Rachel smiled at the younger woman.

Constance pulled back a little. "That really scares me," she said in an awed voice.

"We will both be married. That is a good thing, not something to run from." Rachel felt a little misgiving in declaring such a strong statement to the girl for she did have concerns about her marriage to Jolcum. Men could be fickle when it came to the one, they are marring as to differing expectations and behaviors than what was experienced in a courtship. She had seen that in some of the other women but Felix had basically been the same in courtship and marriage. She realized it might not be the same this time or even for Constance when Daniel approved the suitor.

Constance sensed a change in Rachel. She asked, "But you are thinking something else?"

"We will talk more tomorrow," Rachel answered. "It is too new to me also."

With warm hugs, the two women parted.

Jolcum enjoyed the privileges of a freed man as Daniel had stated. However, his housing was with the Legionnaires and his horse was in the last of the stables used by the Legionnaires. He was required to have an escort within the castle and to many places without. It was politely explained that would help him as he learned about his new resident kingdom.

He knew that he was being watched. His entourage had been waylaid before they left the kingdom and relieved them of the gifts. He paid them for their labors and sent them back to their homes. Several elected to stay with their personage even though they would not be free men. They weren't free men in their home kingdom either, so it seemed not to be an issue.

After many hours of soul searching, a frank discussion with the Friar and another with her cousin Daniel, Lady Rachel was resigned to the marriage without any more discussion. She had kept her silence around Constance until the Princess in her usual intensity told her that she was hiding something from her, Constance. An argument went unresolved until Lady Rachel left in tears. A repentant Constance sought her out asking for forgiveness for her selfish accusation.

Jolcum met with Lady Rachel in the gardens late one afternoon. She was waiting. "It is best we get to know each other," he offered sitting on a bench several feet away. Two Legionnaires discreetly lingered nearby just out of hearing.

Lady Rachel looked at the older but fair-faced man sitting near her. "It has been . . ." and she decided not to finish the sentence. His expression was kind and gentle.

"You are confused?" he asked.

She almost laughed and her smile seemed forced. "Rather unexpected," she said.

"I would have liked to have approached you without the edict by Daniel but being in a compromised position, I had to accept how he told you."

"Compromised?"

"Yes, I was watching you and the Princess from a tree in the woods when you stopped for your picnic."

Lady Rachel looked at him. "Why?"

Jolcum stared down at his hands. "I saw you briefly in passing when I approached the Chancellor as a suitor for your beloved Constance."

"So, I am second choice?" she spat out at him unlike the normal gentle Rachel.

"Oh, no, my dear. I realized that the age differences between the Princess and me would be a barrier. I had heard that her Lady, of Royal blood, was also single due to widowhood." Jolcum paused to let his words sink into Lady Rachel's mind. "I cannot marry a commoner, as it is forbidden in my kingdom for me to marry below my rank."

The two sat for a long time in silence. He studied her mature face while she twisted her fingers on her lap.

"You were spying on us from a tree?" It was as though that part had just suddenly awakened Lady Rachel's mind. "Like a young lad might do?" She was looking at him.

"And I might say," Jolcum took her last two statements as a willingness to talk with him, "I was caught red faced just as a lad might be." His face broke into a smile. "Scared, fearing for my life, and secretly glad to be brought back as a prisoner to stand before the Chancellor and declare my desire for you."

Rachel broke out into laughter as she thought of the man sitting on the other bench acting just like a lad, a lad in budding love. Then she amended her thought, *a man in love*. She blushed and turned her face away hoping to hide the unexpected feelings that were sweeping over her.

"It is best you leave the garden now," she said when she felt she could speak evenly.

Jolcum bowed and walked away. His heart was singing. He had seen her reaction. One of the Legionnaires accompanied him.

Lady Rachel hurried in the other direction to the Royal Chapel hoping that the Friar was present.

"My dear daughter," Friar Joseph said after she had told him the story. "You are wrestling far too much about being obedient to the Chancellor's decree."

Rachel looked up at the Friar at whose knees she was sitting. "I am so confused."

"And afraid?" he asked back.

She didn't answer. The question was unfair or was it. *I have had much life experience, and I am afraid? Yes, I am afraid,* she finally admitted to herself. *All this time, I thought I was to be the strong one, alone.*

Friar Joseph was perplexed with her silence. He resorted to praying touching the beads at his waist. After the silence continued, he interrupted his prayers. "Talk to our Lady Mary," he said softly. "She knows your fear."

Rachel stood and went to where the Blessed Virgin statue with flowers at her feet stood in silence. She knelt down and wept. After a while, she raised her head. She was smiling.

The Friar, deep in intercession for Lady Rachel, did not notice until she rose up and whispered a 'thank you' as she left the chapel.

Sixth Son

*T*he Royal Court was in excitement. From the kingdom to the north, the youngest son of six sons had expressed the desire to meet with the Chancellor. It was to be an event of high ceremony as a state visit, one kingdom to another. The late autumn was unusually warm and the crops had been exceedingly good. This was another reason for countrywide festivals.

Frederick was a frequent visitor with the Chancellor and sometimes the Princess. Although neither man suggested that this young Prince might be the future husband for Constance, there was much speculation. When the rumors began to flow that it was a done agreement, the Chancellor issued an edict under pain of severe punishment for the topic to be discussed by anyone.

Of course, in the privacy of Constance's chambers, Lady Rachel and Constance whispered excitedly about the upcoming state visit. Constance seemed to be more rebellious than she had been in years, threatening to run away or at least hide until after the state visit. Lady Rachel cajoled, begged, and even threatened to tell Daniel of Constance's plans if she should attempt to go through with them.

After one arduous argument, Lady Rachel walked out determined to let her cousin know of the constant stress and misbehavior of Constance. The younger woman caught up with her just before she reached the Throne Room and begged her not to tell on her.

Their discussion drew the attention of others outside the Throne Room. The escorting Legionnaires moved them into an alcove and admonished each to lower their voices. Lady Rachel complied while Constance stood sulking. "Let them know!" she said.

Lady Rachel turned away with her escort. She quietly went to her chambers in tears both for herself and for the rebelliousness of Constance. The gruff voiced Legionnaire held Constance's hand firm in place on his arm as he made his way out into the Royal Gardens. He didn't stop walking until he had reached the statue of the Angel. "Princess," he said quietly, "I am grieved in how you are behaving."

The young woman had not resisted his strong-arm move to get her away from the congestion near the Throne Room. She stood still for a moment staring at nothing. *What is wrong with me,* she began to berate herself.

As though she had said it aloud, the soft gruff voice continued. "Selfish child is how you are acting."

She found herself nodding. "That is what the Friar would say," she murmured.

The Legionnaire realized he had been talking to her without permission. "A thousand pardons, my Princess. I should not be speaking."

She looked at him and quickly looked away. He was crestfallen over his impropriety. She sat down on one of the benches to think. It was a dilemma, his speaking without permission but if she told it, her part would have to be told also. After a long time, she spoke. "I suppose we both need to confess our misdeeds to the Friar. He will know what to do."

The Legionnaire was almost as frightened of the Friar as he was of the Chancellor. He nodded reluctantly for at least the Princess was not blaming him for the whole affair that would have led to serious discipline and pain for him.

Constance was very silent after they had found the Friar and each admitted to their misdeeds. She had seen the fear in her Legionnaire, something new to her. She had always thought of the Legionnaires as fearless and bold. Her escort was anything but that before the Friar. No wonder he had always stayed outside the Chapel when he escorted her there. He was terrified of the power inside the Chapel. It made a profound impression on her.

Daniel had heard of the ruckus in the alcove. He stopped to see Lady Rachel who was mostly mute about what happened. He went to see his niece. He did not bother with formalities at Constance's chamber for those things that Lady Rachel told him incensed him. The ladies of the chamber fell back in awe when he simply burst in without knocking. Giselle read the ire on his face and signaled the women to retreat to the backmost room. Once there with them, she sat on a stool blocking the door and wept. They huddled and wondered at what was transpiring in the other rooms.

Constance expected her uncle's arrival after she talked with the Friar. She was a little startled that he did not follow protocol. It was a clue to his anger. She was sitting in the library, holding a book but not seeing the pages.

For what seemed like an eternity, Daniel stood in the doorway of the library. He looked at her, and she kept her eyes downcast. He closed the door behind him. It seemed to echo the sound of doom to her ears. "Come here," he said. His voice was low.

Constance stood and obeyed. She stopped a foot in front of him waiting for his discipline. She did not look up at him.

When he moved, she instinctively cringed. He wrapped his arms around her instead and pulled her close to him. She could hear his heart beating. For a full minute, he held her close to him before he said, "I love you Constance, even when I am sorely disappointed in you."

She waited for a pinch or a blow that didn't come. He cradled her in his arms. "Oh, my dear child, it has been a rough road for both of us." His embrace tightened as she realized he was crying. She had never seen her uncle cry although she had been told that she had caused him many tears. The peacefulness of the embrace with his tears triggered her tears. Soon she was sobbing and clinging to her uncle.

"Let's talk," he said when he had finally stilled his tears and dried hers. He guided her to a chair and pulled up another. "The Legionnaire told me what happened."

"He didn't have to," Constance interrupted. "I told him that it had been my fault. Ask the Friar, he will tell you that I forgave him."

"As the Chancellor, I am the superior commander of the Legionnaires. He recognized his disobedience to a member of the royal household and confessed it to me. It is part of his allegiance and fidelity to me."

Constance was looking earnestly into the face of her uncle. "But I caused it," she repeated. Then a look of pain crossed her face. Her uncle had used that word 'fidelity'. "What are you going to do to him?"

Daniel saw her distress. "I sent him to my private rooms until I could get this all straightened out."

His answer did not give her any peace. "Then what?" she persisted.

Her uncle did not answer. After an agonizing pause, he replied," I think I might let the Queen decide that,"

The words just passed over Constance's head. She nodded because that usually covered long silences.

"He would make a good addition to the Queen's staff since she does listen to him, even when he is not supposed to speak."

The word Queen confused Constance. She looked closer at her uncle's face. *What is he talking about?*

He said, "You will be the Queen soon."

"You intend that I marry this man coming from the kingdom to the north?" she asked her voice giving away her lack of calmness.

"I don't know," Daniel said and stretched his legs as though sitting as the King all day had left him tense and tired. He waited for her to formulate at least one question before he said more. He knew she had many for Lady Rachel had told him.

"Please, Sire," Constance retreated to the formal title. "Tell me about our expected visitor."

He wanted to chuckle but he would not laugh at her seriousness.

"Nathaniel is the sixth son of seven children of King Adrian. He seems to be the only one who has any sense also. His older brothers are quarreling with each other over who is going to rule which parts of the kingdom when their father passes. His sister has retreated to the sanctuary of the church for her protection and the common people are aware of the discord in the royal family."

"Why doesn't King Adrian stop it?" Constance asked forgetting that it was the sixth sensible son who was coming to visit.

"When a man gets old and his progeny are fighting for superiority, it is easier to let them fight, and possibly the best man will win. If not, the strongest will win. King Adrian is ailing so the fight for the potential throne is more out the open. I understand that the commoners are become restless also.

"Nathaniel asked to come for a state visit. He is more diplomatic than his brutish brothers. He also sees that the throne will never be his as the sixth son does not have much of a chance without killing off the others. That is not a pleasant way to become king." Daniel laughed remembering his own brother usurping of the throne.

"So, when will this sixth son, Nathaniel, be here?"

"Frederick has set the date for the 6th of next month. Appropriate for a sixth son, don't you think?"

Constance counted the number of days until the 6th. "Ten days from now?"

"Yes, and he will be here about ten days unless . . ." Daniel let the sentence hanging unfinished.

She looked at her uncle. "Unless?" She knew the answer but was afraid to say it herself.

"We will see," her uncle gave a less than acceptable answer.

"Are you going to decree a marriage for me like you did for Lady Rachel?"

The Chancellor took a deep breath. "I am not sure that would go over very well with the Princess." He was watching her reaction from the corner of his eye.

"Umm," Constance was buying time to think of a good response. "Probably not, I hear that she is difficult at times."

Her response caught him unexpectedly. He almost laughed aloud. He turned to face her more directly. "I expect the Princess to say the right words at the right time." His eyes met hers.

She felt the sting and yet the thrill of facing her uncle's authority head on. She nodded, fearful that any answer she might make now would be the wrong one.

The ten days passed with astounding rapidity. Constance, under Giselle's eye, inspected her royal gowns and made herself as ready as anyone can for the unknown. Lady Rachel stayed close by quietly encouraging the Princess to relax and be herself.

"I am not sure that Uncle Daniel wants me to be myself," she confided in her Lady. "After all, myself is so prone to do the wrong things at the very moment that everyone will notice."

"That, my dear Constance, is why I will be your ever-present Lady."

"Did my uncle tell you that?" Constance looked sharply at her friend.

"He did not have to tell me, we all know." She chuckled. "Your behavior is not a secret."

Constance dropped her head. "Now you are going to make me feel ashamed."

"That would be a new thing for you," Lady Rachel noted.

The younger woman asked, "Which, ashamed or feelings? I have felt both of late more than I wish to remember especially when kneeling in the Chapel with the Friar.   Lady Rachel smiled. "It must be a sign you are maturing." She laughed and ducked the small pillow Constance threw at her.

"And tomorrow, I must act like a lady," Constance put on a serious face. "Is there laughter in marriage? I dare say, I shall shrivel and dry up like a prune if there isn't."

"Anyone who grows up as the sixth son surely must laugh a lot at the antics of his older brothers as they vie for the same throne." Lady Rachel was carefully replacing the most formal of Constance's gowns into the room where they were kept. "I have seen nothing of a wedding gown in all these dresses."

Constance shrieked, "Wedding gown! Is that what you have been looking for all afternoon? I thought you were just making sure the dressmaker has sewn up all the seams!"

The two women, the Queen-to-be and Lady Rachel fell into peals of laughter in each other's arms.

A sharp flash and a clap of thunder woke those who were still asleep early the next morning. The whole castle seemed to be in mourning while sheets of rain fell. Inside, the Throne Room was brightly lit but outside a storm persisted.

Constance stared out the closed windows of the Morning Room. Word came midmorning that the visiting Prince had elected to stay outside of the city until the rains stopped.

"What if they never stop?"

"The rains, my Princess?" Lady Rachel had stopped by.

"And he goes away because of the rains," Constance answered gloomily.

"Provision has been made for him and his entourage. Tents are erected in the meadow for his horses. I don't think the rains will keep him away long," Rachel responded.

"What do I wear today, something that will not be ruined by the rain?"

"You could wear one of those dresses you wore when you were helping at St. Stephen's."

"They are all too small now, and besides I gave them away to some of the girls there." Constance scowled. "Rachel, how about that old blue dress without the lace on the collar and wrists?"

"If you don't want to be noticed," Rachel responded absentmindedly.

"And you can wear that dull brown one you have," Constance answered back.

Rachel looked at the Princess. "What are you thinking about?"

Constance laughed softly. "If he is stuck out there because of the rains . . ."

"No!" Rachel stated emphatically.

Constance continued as if Rachel had said nothing. "We will go out as some of the women of the town and offer our services to the Royal visitor. I am sure there is much work for women to do in the encampment. Then I can see him first before he knows that I am the princess. You know there will be women from the town offering to help."

Rachel stood for a moment looking at the younger woman and caught the excitement that now bubbled out of Constance. The young woman would be difficult to control if she had to just sit and wait. *Why not let the girl have one last adventure?* Rachel knew she was not thinking rationally and that the Chancellor would disapprove. "Let me see what I can do," she looked at the princess and grinned.

Within the hour, Lady Rachel had a small conspiracy formed for Constance to the visiting Prince's temporary encampment incognito. Ian got wind of the irregular adventure. Rachel convinced him to go with them. Reluctantly he agreed when he realized that the Princess would do it with or without adequate protection. The party included one Legionnaire loyal to Constance, Ian, Jolcum, Rachel and Constance.

Slipping out under the cover of the rain, the party quickly looked bedraggled as they crossed the streets of the town going toward the far edge. The dresses of the two women soon looked like the everyday peasants. Their dresses were spattered by mud in the streets from passing riders or wagons.

Playing the role of eldest brother, Jolcum was astounded at Lady Rachel's resourcefulness. They carried baskets of freshly baked bread from one of the shops in town which they distributed to a few of the visitors as they made their way deeper and deeper into the enclave of visiting Prince. Constance, posing as a merchant girl, offered her last two loaves as a gift to Prince Nathaniel. He thanked her and the others for their hospitality and pressed a gold coin into Constance's hand. She stood awestruck until her two brothers, Ian and the disguised Legionnaire urged their 'sisters' to get back to the bakery shop before their father missed them. They bowed awkwardly and headed back across town. Ian and the Legionnaire carried Constance by the elbows between them.

In the royal stables, some of the ladies in waiting from Constance's Chamber had dry clean clothing for the women.

Giselle was wringing her hands when Constance finally arrived back safely. "Your uncle wants to see you!" Quickly, any traces of mud were removed from Constance and her hair was done up as though she had just taken a bath.

"When did he ask for me?"

"You were just gone," Giselle said as she made her last inspection before sending the girl off to see her uncle.

"Does he know?" Constance asked.

"No, I don't think so," Giselle answered.

"What did you tell him?"

"On my word, nothing,"

"Did he believe you?"

"He is the Chancellor," Giselle said before sending the girl on her way

Take me by the Royal Chapel," Constance ordered the Legionnaire who was escorting her.

Friar Joseph was not there. She knelt before the Virgin Mary statue and asked for her protection.

"Where have you been?" The Chancellor stood looking at his niece in his best authoritative manner.

"Sire, I was in the Royal Chapel," Constance murmured,

"Not when I was there," he retorted.

Constance met his eyes for a moment then looked down.

"What do you want of me?"

"The truth," he said.

"I was out in the stables. I am restless with the weather being so . . ."

She heard a tiny snap of his fingers and glanced up.

His eyes were boring into hers.

A shudder passed across her face.

"I ask for forgiveness, uncle. I went to see the Prince."

"Did he know it was you?"

"No, Sire, I was dressed as a peasant merchant girl. I gave him two loaves of bread."

"Were you alone?" his voice was not as fierce as she had expected.

"No, Sire, there were five of us."

"No harm came to you?"

"No, Sire."

Daniel turned and sat down and indicated the chair near him for Constance. For a long while they sat in silence.

"Whose idea was this?"

"Mine, Sire," Constance stated.

"And Lady Rachel went with you?"

"Yes, Sire, but it was my idea in the first place."

"Who else went?" Daniel knew that he was pressing Constance to see if she would tell him all of the truth.

"Ian, Jolcum and one of the Legionnaires."

"Certainly not with their crests on their shoulders."

"They wore the rags of the poorer stable hands."

"Did you steal the bread?"

The shocked look on Constance's face answered that question but he waited to see what she would say. "No, Sire, we used a few coins to buy it."

Daniel nodded. He turned to look at her. "I don't approve of what you did, but it came to no harm. What do you suppose I should do with Lady Rachel, Jolcum, the Legionnaire and the lad Ian?"

"Delay judgment, Sire. Let the new Queen handle that when she comes to the throne."

"That does not seem wise." Daniel tapped his left foot as he often did when trying to decide on something. "What if they decide to continue their misbehavior and put the Queen at risk? I should think it would be wiser to make examples of them."

"Then start with me," Constance said quietly.

The quick gasp by her uncle alerted her that he had not expected her response. The silence between them went on for a long time. "The Queen can handle it better than I," he said.

"Thank you, uncle." Constance stood up and went to Daniel and bowed. "I will be just." She smiled and kissed him on the cheek.

Like a little girl, she skipped back to her chambers, rejoicing and thanking God for answered prayers. "Oh," she said when she was close to her rooms, "I need to go to the Chapel and thank the Virgin for her help." The escort and she made swift time to the Chapel where Constance knelt and rejoiced in the assurance that the days to come were to be even better days. "Oh, and Mary, thank you for the handsome man that Prince is!"

Daniel knelt in his own private rooms and thanked God for the coming days and for Constance. He was satisfied that she was nearly ready for the Throne.

"Sire, Jolcum is asking to see you." Daniel nodded at his private servant.

"Show him in."

Jolcum knelt in submission before the Chancellor and waited for him to give him freedom to speak.

Daniel nodded. "I know. Under other circumstances, the whole thing could have been a serious offense. Constance will soon be Queen, and as Queen, she will dispense any justice that needs to be done."

Jolcum bowed his head. "She will be a strong Queen. Her determination is her power."

Neither man had mentioned the event but they were talking about the same thing. "Thank you, Jolcum, and may you enjoy your wife as well when you are married."

The rain stopped the next day. The celebration was put off for two days more until the mud had dried. The sun was shining brightly and all was in readiness. It was as though the delay allowed for a more intense and a better prepared for celebration.

Constance was nervous. "What if he should recognize me as the one who brought him the bread?"

Lady Rachel was trying with several others of the ladies-in-waiting to fasten the long series of buttons in correct sequence. "Just stand still please," Lady Rachel said as she undid two buttons that were out of sequence.

The young woman sighed. "This is so tedious."

Rachel from her kneeling position at the girl's feet laughed. "You will get used to it in time."

"Will not!" Constant came back quickly.

"Shall I call Daniel," Rachel said as she stood up directly in front of her friend.

"No," the girl murmured. "He would only get in the way."

"That is an interesting excuse to avoid him and his discipline," Rachel said to Constance as the other women had left the room.

"Can I sit now?"

Rachel arranged the full gown carefully as Constance sat on the indicated stool.

"How much longer?" she asked.

"I can hear the crowds in the distance. They are louder now than they were so he has probably entered the city.

"What if he recognizes me or doesn't want me?"

Rachel laughed. "You asked that first part before."

"I know," the young Princess murmured. "My thinking is so mixed up today."

Lady Rachel laughed again just as it was announced that Friar Joseph was in the entry room. "An answer to prayer," Lady Rachel said mostly to herself.

Constance walked out into that room. Friar Joseph rose from where he had been sitting and bowed.

The younger woman was stunned. Never in all the encounters with the Friar had he ever bowed to her. She had always been the one to kneel. She felt strange in this change of positions. Only Lady Rachel had seen it. She glanced at Rachel and saw the awed look on her friend's face as the woman left the room.

"Friar?" Constance said softly.

"You represent our kingdom today." he said. "This is a day of great rejoicing even as the approach of Prince Nathaniel is bringing great shouts of joy. Most know without being told that the kingdom will be greater than before by his visit."

It took Constance a few minutes to understand what the Friar was saying to her. "Oh," she said in amazement. She looked down at her shaking hands, "I am so afraid." In a flash, she remembered the first time she had looked into this Friar's eyes. "I think I have said that to you before," she smiled wanly.

"As a child," he answered.

"Inside, you know that I am still a little child."

A courier from the Throne Room interrupted the slight nod by the Friar. "Princess, the Chancellor wants you."

Constance looked at the Legionnaire standing ready at the door. *A faithful man*, she thought as she placed her hand on the now familiar spot on his arm.

Daniel was dressed in splendid attire that proclaimed he was the ruler of the kingdom. He smiled when Constance appeared. *Next ruler*, he thought. *She carries herself well.* He smiled at her and offered her his arm as they made their way to where Prince Nathaniel would dismount and the formal of amenities of state would be exchanged. Constance would just be in the background for most of the ceremonies, except for the formal introduction.

Impressed, Nathaniel rode his jet-black horse through the city to the cheering populous. When they came to the plaza where the Cathedral stood, he dismounted and went inside to kneel before the altar. The crowds outside stood in hushed silence while he was inside. It had been years since the kingdom had seen a ruler kneel at the altar.

When the sounds of the crowds had hushed, Constance looked at her uncle. "What is going on," she asked.

A few words were exchanged with the various couriers, pages and Legionnaires.

"He stopped at the Cathedral to give thanks for his travels and this visit."

Constance felt faint. Friar Joseph was at her elbow. "He is the one, Princess. He is a gift from God."

Her look into the Friar's eyes did not have to have words. It said what she always said to him, *I am so afraid.*

"God is with you," he whispered.

The roar of the crowd began again. Prince Nathaniel was on the last leg of his entrance to the kingdom. His splendid black mount seemed to dance as he came into sight. His protecting guardsmen fell back as the Legionnaires on horses moved in closer to him. Constance felt a shock when she realized that one of the Legionnaires was Ian.

In front of the stone porch that had been erected just for this visit, the visiting Prince halted. A crier formally announced his name and Kingdom. His horse seemed to bow even as rider on its back acknowledged the presence of the Chancellor and other Royalty.

After they had retired to the Throne Room, where Constance had a preferential seat at the right hand of her uncle, there were still sounds of great rejoicing by the crowds outside. Between the exchange of formal gifts, actually quite small by comparison to some others who had made formal visits, and the small talk that seemed to be exchanged between the two men, the things of the court seemed to move along rather slowly.

At one point, her uncle turned to her and said, "If you are tired, my Princess, you may withdraw from this tedious formality.

Constance had been watching Prince Nathaniel out of the corner of her eyes, trying not to stare. *Sixth son* her mind interjected. Her faithful Legionnaire stepped forward. It was obvious this had been a formal dismissal even though the Chancellor had not said it in that manner. She stood, placing her hand on the offered arm. Aware that everyone was watching her, she walked in what she hoped was an elegant manner through the arches that led back to her rooms.

Lady Rachel and Giselle were waiting like two old women for the latest gossip. "Well?" Rachel asked.

Constance submitted to the unbuttoning of her elegant gown. "May I just step out of it without undoing all the buttons?" The nodding heads by her attendants agreed and when it seemed loose enough for her to step out of, she did.

She reclined for a while on her bed until it was time to dress for the formal dinner and the stroll in the royal gardens afterwards with the visiting Prince.

The Chancellor and Prince Nathaniel were eyeing each other cautiously. Daniel had all the information that his friend Frederick had told him about the younger man. Likewise, Nathaniel had spent time with his emissaries learning about the Princess Constance.

"It is agreeable with you to marry my niece?"

Nathaniel had practiced the long pause before answers on the recommendation of Frederick, no less. "Sire, I would like a face to face meeting with her alone before I consent."

Daniel looked at the young man. "Did someone give you that advice?"

A beautiful young smile crossed the young man's face. "My Mother, Sire." What he didn't also say was that Frederick had recommended the same.

"A good mother." Daniel said not asking it as a question.

"Yes, Sire, she is grieved by the quarrels my brothers are in."

"And how do you feel about them?" Daniel asked.

Nathaniel didn't say anything for a few minutes. "I am confused by their vehemence and hatred."

"As you surely should be. Such behavior can lead to the fall of a kingdom."

Again, silence broke into their conversation.

"There are a few things you need to know about the Princess."

Nathaniel wanted to grin but he remained neutral. His spies had told him much, so there was probably very little he did not know. "Yes, Sire?" he answered after a suitable pause.

"She is very strong willed. She was spoiled during her childhood years. Since I have been on the throne, I have disciplined her."

"Does she accept discipline," Nathaniel was shocked when the words came out of his mouth.

Daniel had been looking across the room as though he had unseen notes that he was reading. He looked at the younger man. "I have had to use more discipline than what I wanted to use."

Nathaniel saw the pain in the older man's eyes. He nodded. His spies had told him that also. "So," the younger man said, deliberately, "She hates you now?"

Daniel almost missed the glint of humor in the Prince's comment.

"You have done your research well, I can see," the Chancellor answered back avoiding the question. "My question is", Daniel stopped speaking. "My statement is," he corrected, will you be able to love her for she will be a formidable Queen?"

Prince Nathaniel sat with his head bowed as he thought of his answer. "I cannot truthfully say that until I have had some time to know her. I understand fully my position as a possible husband for the Princess, and I understand that I am giving up my rights to the kingdom I have lived in all my life and must submit to the authority of the ruler of this kingdom, whether it is you or the Queen.

"As a man and a husband, there are other lines of authority also in life as you well understand in taking the leadership over your niece. She is in obedience to you both as the leader of this kingdom and to you as her only living relative. Likewise, there will be a similar duality for me, submission to the Queen as ruler of this kingdom and her submission to me as her husband."

Daniel sighed. *This man is very intelligent and educated.* "That could make life very hard for you."

"Or her," Nathaniel replied.

"Yes."

Silence reigned again.

"I need time alone with her," Nathaniel restated. "Only then will I be able to say to you that I am agreeable for a marriage."

What a deep thinker Prince Nathaniel is. What a pity his kingdom will not ever benefit from his thinking! The Chancellor nodded. "That time will start tonight after the banquet. She will show you the Royal Gardens."

"And her ever present Lady or escorts?"

"You will be alone."

After the banquet, the Chancellor turned to Princess Constance sitting at his right hand. "Go take a rest in the Royal Gardens."

Constance stared at her uncle but only briefly because his word had been stated with authority. She had not spoken with Nathaniel during the meal as he was seated on the left side of the Chancellor.

Lady Rachel, seated beside her, started to rise to be in attendance to her when the Chancellor whispered a sharp 'no'. The faithful Legionnaire stepped forward smartly and offered the Princess his arm. He had been instructed earlier by the Chancellor to escort and then remain guarding the entrance to the garden from intruders after the Prince had joined her.

Constance quivered from excitement and fear as she sat on the designated stone seat. As the evening was brisk, she had donned a cloak with the Royal Crest before going out to the Royal Garden. Minutes later she heard footsteps approaching. It was difficult to remain seated so great was her urge to run away. *I want to run and hide* she thought as the footsteps came closer.

Prince Nathaniel stepped into the circle of light from one of the discretely placed torches that lit the garden. He stopped and considered her from a far before coming closer and bowing before her. "Princess Constance," his voice caressed her ears.

"Prince Nathaniel," she acknowledged.

"It is strange, but for a moment, I thought I had met you earlier during the rains."

Constance felt a cold chill run down her spine and she pulled her cloak closer. "But we just met today," she answered.

"A young peasant woman came with her brothers and sister and brought me two loaves of bread," Nathaniel was now seated on the other bench close to her. "They came in the rains to offer me and my entourage hospitality. I found that very endearing." Nathaniel paused watching Constance's face closely. "But then I am mistaken, you are not the girl. Alas, I would like to thank her again for our bread had gotten wet in the rains and we so badly needed some."

Constance had ceased to look at his face but was studying the way his clothes fit him, the movement of his hands when he spoke. Anything but to look into those eyes which were so eagerly searching her face. "I am so glad that our people were so sensitive to your needs," she said, daring to look into his face.

"Yes," he said. "I asked the Chancellor for this private meeting as he has told you."

Constance only nodded afraid her voice would give her emotions away.

"The Chancellor is an exact and fiercely tough man," the prince smiled. "His demands for my fidelity, allegiance and love for you, my Princess, are hard to meet. He expects love even before I know you."

Constance swallowed hard. She knew of her uncle's fierce demands upon her, his constant eye on her maturity. She had not expected it to include the man she was to marry. "The Chancellor, my uncle, has been a stern taskmaster. You may have heard of my earlier childhood."

Nathaniel nodded, a smile still playing on his face. "Your exploits have been tales told even abroad although I suspect they have been embellished by the story tellers."

Constance let her head fall as she looked at her hands still clutching the cloak close to her. "Do those tales worry you?" she asked in a maturity that was beginning to become more comfortable.

It was Nathaniel's turn to look away briefly. "No."

A comfortable silence settled between then.

"Will you show me the gardens?"

"Yes," she said standing. She was glad for the diversion from the intensity of the conversation.

He offered his arm and she responded as though it was natural for her. They took the path in front of them. At its intersection, she turned them into a darker one although the torches shed a gentle light over the complete gardens.

When they came across a statue, Constance would call it by name and explain its purpose in the garden. Suddenly they were in the center where the Guardian Angel stood, wings unfurled.

Nathaniel stopped in awe. "Beautiful," he whispered and turned to look at Constance. Her eyes glittered in the light of the torch set at the angel's feet. "So strong, he is."

Constance turned and looked at Nathaniel and said, "He?"

"Angels are male because of their strength."

She had taken a step away and was studying the statue.

"Feel the wings," Nathaniel had stepped closer to the statue.

"I was told to never climb on the statue," slipped out of Constance's mouth.

"Here," he reached an arm around her and raised her up on her tiptoes, "Touch."

She did.

His hand had guided hers to the edge of the stone wings. "Strength, protecting strength." Letting her back down on her feet, he guided her to a bench and sat down facing her.

Constance could feel her heart pounding from his closeness as he had supported her to touch the wing. She concentrated on keeping her breathing regular. She had never felt like she felt at that moment; fear, strength, and a desire for another touch.

Nathaniel was speaking but she was not hearing as she searched her mind for why she was so distracted. He seemed to be waiting for her to speak and she did not know what he had said.

"I am sorry," she murmured.

The pleasant face of the young Prince did not change. "I asked: what did you do with the gold coin?"

Her gasp confirmed what Nathaniel had known. She said, looking into the face of this man, "You know!"

He nodded.

"How?"

"Answer my question first." His eyes were boring into her eyes and her heart.

She covered her face as she felt a blush rise to her cheeks. "It is in a secret place," she answered.

Her statement did not exactly answer the question but Nathaniel was satisfied. "My special ones followed you back to the royal stable." He answered her question.

She nodded her head and remained silent, as did he. For a time, they sat. She was not uncomfortable and she found that she was not as cold as she was earlier. She looked up when he stirred. He was watching her.

"My beloved," he whispered as a breeze passed through the branches of the evergreen tree near her.

"Song of Songs," she whispered in return.

"You know the scripture?"

"Friar has been teaching me about love and marriage," she answered back.

"I also am studying that book."

"What have you told my uncle, the Chancellor?"

Nathaniel looked down. "I am ashamed to say, my beloved, I have not given him an answer."

"Why?" Constance was surprised as she had thought his whole purpose in coming to their kingdom was to be wed to her.

"I asked him for time alone with you instead. He had asked me a hard question and I reminded him that the answer was a difficult one to make."

His statement made sense but then again, she was expected to obey if her uncle betrothed her to Nathaniel. *Why does he have the right of reservation?*

As though Nathaniel heard her thought, he spoke up. "You shall have absolute authority over every subject in your kingdom, including me. However, in God's plan, the husband has authority over his wife. It is similar but not the same as your uncle having authority over you as a niece and also authority over everyone in the kingdom."

Constance sat for a while pondering what he had said. "Even to marry you, I have to answer to my uncle, first as my uncle and to the Chancellor, also my uncle, because he is also the Chancellor. It seems a bit lopsided and again, it isn't." She sighed and looked to see of Nathaniel had heard her.

"My beloved," Nathaniel had used that statement for the third time. "I will never attempt to wrestle the throne away from you. It is part of fidelity to the throne as it exists to remain faithful to that pledge."

"It is treason otherwise," Constance murmured. She had understood that since she was very little. Even when Daniel had come back to the castle, he had still remained in fidelity to the throne.

Nathaniel nodded. "But as your husband, in the private things of marriage, I must be the authority." He offered her his arm and she rose.

"What are you going to say to my uncle?" she asked as they took a different path back to the entrance of the garden.

"We will talk again tomorrow."

"With my uncle?" she asked.

"No, you and I."

Constance had a restless night. Giselle had tried rubbing the Princess' back until the young woman ordered her away. She sent for Lady Rachel.

"She will be asleep," Giselle complained.

"I want her!" was the terse reply.

Rachel came wrapped in a cloak. She looked at the disheveled bedding and smiled. "You want to talk?"

After the others had retired, the two women sat in the semi-darkened sleeping chamber and talked until near dawn. When Constance finally fell into bed exhausted, Rachel asked, "What are you going to tell the Chancellor when he sends for you?"

"I am infirmed," she said as she closed her eyes.

Lady Rachel instructed the ladies of the chamber to honor the Princess' sleep before retiring again to her own chambers.

Betrothed

Nathaniel poured over the Song of Songs. He sought out the Friar in the Royal Chapel and listened to his heart most of all. Constance was lovely to look at, spirited, and aware of the necessity of obedience. Still, he hesitated to talk again with the Chancellor. It was too soon.

He sat down at the small desk in the guest chambers with the holy book open before him. He penned a short note, not original, but heart felt.

You are as a flower in bloom.
You are my beloved. Nathaniel

He sought out the gardener for a late blooming flower and sent his courier to deliver the written message and flower to the Princess' chamber.

Constance stared at the carefully scripted note and the lone flower with it. She had not been awake long.

"If you hurry, you can be ready for the late afternoon tea," Giselle urged her. A series of notes had flowed between the Chancellor and her life-long lady. He had been concerned when it was reported that Constance was still in bed. He urged that she be up in time for the special tea in the afternoon.

Constance yawned as she clutched the note and flower to her breast. It wasn't a yawn of boredom, but just one of those things that happens when you sleep late.

"What should I wear?" Giselle had anticipated the question and two gowns were laid out.

"The deep rose one," Constance chose while letting one of the other women begin the tedious task of untangling her long hair that had not been bound up when she finally went to sleep.

"Ouch," she protested and took the brush from the girl's hand. She began a more vigorous attack on her hair and soon it was looking normal.

A demure Princess arrived on time at the tea. Prince Nathaniel arrived shortly thereafter as was the normal plan when two are first seeing each other.

He bowed to the Chancellor and again to Princess Constance. He noticed that she had placed his flower in among her locks of hair, held securely by a diamond-studded hairpin. "My beloved," he murmured to her out of hearing of the others in the room. Constance lightly blushed. She had worn extra powder on her face in case of a blush. She was glad she had taken Lady Rachel's advice.

Jolcum arrived and sought out Lady Rachel after the required greetings of the Chancellor, Constance and Nathaniel. "You look sleepy," he said to Rachel. They both laughed for she had already told him of her nightlong visit with Constance.

"And she looks lovely," Lady Rachel answered with a nod toward the future Queen.

After the light sandwiches, finger cakes and tea were consumed; the men stepped into the next room for something stronger. Nathaniel was accustomed to this ritual. He made small talk with the several men before excusing himself. He had an appointment to keep with Constance.

She was waiting at the edge of the garden with her faithful Legionnaire. Nathaniel nodded a dismissal to the man and placed her hand on his arm. They went to the Angel statue first. "See, he does have male attributes," he said as they paused.

Constance shook her head. I was always taught that angels were feminine."

"The long hair?" Nathaniel challenged back.

She shrugged her shoulders. She led him through other parts of the garden, again stopping and talking about the various statues. "I love the sculpture," she said casually. "Unfortunately, they tell me that women do not sculpt."

Nathaniel looked at her with a glint in his eye. "Sit down, my beloved, and let me explain something." She sat on the indicated bench. "Women, with the help of God, sculpt much more perfectly than any man can do in stone." She looked at him with disbelief. He continued. "When a tiny baby is within you, you are sculpting with the Master!"

As she realized what he was saying, her face turned red. No powder could have hidden her blush. "Oh," she said softly as she clasped her hands over her face. "May we always sculpt together with the Master." Nathaniel had now seated himself beside her. Slowly she was beginning to understand.

"Master?" she said softly, "God?"

He nodded and even he felt embarrassed at talking about that part of their life to be. "I told your uncle that I accept his challenge."

"Oh," she said again. Thrill, fear, awe and other feelings she could not explain seemed to squeeze out reality at that moment. She wept.

"Why the tears?" he whispered to her. She only shook her head and sobbed at the gigantic emotion that was overwhelming her. She realized that childhood, and childish things would never be hers again. All the battles she had fought to remain a child were over. Ian was no longer her guide and protector. Nathaniel would be. She probably was weeping for that loss but when Nathaniel placed his arm around her shoulders to support her as she wept, she leaned into his protection.

They sat together for a long time even after she had stopped crying. So long had they sat there that the Legionnaires discretely searched the Royal Gardens to find them. When they did locate them, they tiptoed away as the future Queen sat close to her future husband as they watched the sun begin to set over the meadow where the tents were for Nathaniel's entourage.

Constance found words running through her mind as she turned to look at this man she barely knew. "Welcome, my beloved."

They walked slowly back to the entrance of the Royal Gardens, neither speaking. Constance worried that her tears would be visible. Nathaniel had gently wiped her face until there were no remaining traces of the tears. They stepped into the banquet hall just as dinner was being announced.

He sat on the left of the Chancellor, and Constance on the right. Only Lady Rachel had an inkling of what had happened in the garden.

Afterward, with only the Chancellor present, Constance and Nathaniel had knelt before him in his chambers as he decreed their marriage. Constance had learned the words from Lady Rachel and responded. "Let it be done as you say."

The next day, near midday, the Chancellor stood at the Throne and stated. "Princess Constance and Prince Nathaniel are to be wed in the spring." The two stood flanking him. The crowds roared and soon the city was in celebration for the good news.

Constance went to bed with a headache as Nathaniel made arrangements to send most of his entourage home. He would stay a little longer, and then go home to comfort his mother. A courier had come to say that his father was not expected to live out a fortnight longer. He had no desire to allow his bickering brothers to interfere with his new happiness. The private message from his mother had said, "Stay, it will be less dangerous for you my son. I will wait your visit afterwards."

Winter came with vengeance. Those who did not believe in God said that He was angry over the impending marriage. Sickness was rife through the kingdom with even the Princess and Lady Rachel spending days in bed with a cough and fever. Ian was ill two months before he finally was well. Daniel ignored the symptoms until he collapsed in the Throne Room one day. Constance stepped forward, barely up from her own sick bed.

The Friars were busy day and night, anointing the sick and dying and burying those who succumbed. The children at the monastery died at an alarming rate. When a child survived, Constance made arrangements to send the child back to his or her family. Daniel grumbled until his cough weakened him such that any sound he made set him to coughing. Friar Joseph sat at his bedside day and night.

Nathaniel had gone home after his father's death just long enough to pack up his grieving mother, and slip away in the dark of night. His brothers each had militias and were fighting each other. Nathaniel considered himself fortunate to find a sympathetic commoner who hid him until he could make it across the grueling mountains when the weather permitted. He entrusted his mother to a ship's captain to set sail immediately to his beloved's kingdom. It had cost them dearly in the gold and silver his mother had hidden away when his brothers began their bickering years before.

History records that winter as one of the deadliest ever experienced with multiple deaths due to weather, illness and the fighting in his birth kingdom. Constance's kingdom didn't have the fighting, although the weather and sickness were severe.

Anon! Spring came with a burst of sunshine, abundance of flowers, and the royal wedding!

The End